AVON'S VELVET GLOVE SERIES

"THE VELVET GLOVE SERIES WILL BE-
COME AN EXCITING ALTERNATIVE TO
THE STRAIGHT ROMANCE. ALL OF THE
SENSUALITY AND MAGNETISM OF RO-
MANCES IS THERE AND ALSO THE
'CLIFF-HANGING' TENSENESS OF GOOD
SUSPENSE."

Affaire de Coeur

"IT'S WHAT WE FEEL IS A NEW TREND
IN ROMANTIC FICTION—ROMANTIC
SUSPENSE."

Kathryn Falk,
Romantic Times

"THE VELVET GLOVE LINE IS GEARED
TO ROMANTIC SUSPENSE . . . THE SUR-
VIVAL OF LOVE HOLDS THE READER
IN AS MUCH SUSPENSE AS THE DAN-
GER."

Terri Busch,
Heart Line

Avon Books publishes two new Velvet Glove
books each month. Ask for them at your book-
store.

Velvet Glove

14

Carla Neggers
The Uneven Score

▲ AVON
PUBLISHERS OF BARD, CAMELOT, DISCUS AND FLARE BOOKS

THE UNEVEN SCORE is an original publication of Avon
Books. This work has never before appeared in book form.
This work is a novel. Any similarity to actual persons or
events is purely coincidental.

AVON BOOKS
A division of
The Hearst Corporation
1790 Broadway
New York, New York 10019

Copyright © 1985 by Velvet Glove, Inc. and Carla Neggers
Published by arrangement with Velvet Glove, Inc.
Library of Congress Catalog Card Number: 84-91214
ISBN: 0-380-89665-6

First Avon Printing, February, 1985

AVON TRADEMARK REG. U. S. PAT. OFF. AND IN
OTHER COUNTRIES, MARCA REGISTRADA, HECHO EN
U. S. A.

Printed in the U. S. A.

WFH 10 9 8 7 6 5 4 3 2 1

For Douglas

Prologue

THE telephone rang during Whitney's second hour of practicing études for the French horn. It was March in Schenectady, a dull and dreary time of year. The sap was running, the snow was melting, and Whitney was ensconced on a straight-backed chair in the living room of her little house on the Mohawk River. Her cat, Wolfgang, was stretched out in front of the stone fireplace, the glow of the flames flickering on his orange fur. His ears twitched when the ring of the telephone clashed with the high B-flat Whitney was playing.

"I'm not out of tune," she said, getting up, "the phone is."

Most musicians Whitney knew used answering machines during their practice hours, but she treasured interruptions, often finding a chat with a friend or bill collector refreshing. Especially when practicing études, she thought, especially during March, when life was almost unbearably quiet. She tucked her horn under her arm, picked up the phone, and said hello.

"Whitney," a vaguely familiar voice said, "this is Victoria."

"Victoria?" Whitney frowned thoughtfully. There was a Victoria in the flute section of the Mohawk Valley Community Orchestra, of which Whitney was the conductor, but she was only eighteen. This Victoria sounded older and irrepressibly self-confident and—no, Whitney thought, it couldn't be!

"Is Harry there?" Victoria demanded. "The fink. Has he called?"

Whitney almost dropped her horn. "Victoria Paderevsky!"

"Yes, of course."

7

Victoria Paderevsky was the music director of the newly formed Central Florida Symphony Orchestra and one of the most controversial and brilliant conductors in the world. She was controversial because she was a woman in a man's profession, singularly unattractive, egotistical, and notoriously tyrannical. Her view of her position harked back to the days of Serge Koussevitzky and Arturo Toscanini, when a conductor was lord and master of his musicians, free to be tolerant or intolerant, however he saw fit.

But she was also undeniably brilliant. At age thirty-eight she had an immense repertory of orchestral works, possessed a rare and gifted musical voice, and had led some of the best orchestras in the world during her years as a free-lance conductor. Although early in her career she had served as an assistant conductor with the New York Philharmonic, she had never had a major podium of her own. The offers had just started to come in, but Victoria Paderevsky had decided to accept an offer from a group in Orlando, Florida, to start her own orchestra. Because she had conducted all over the world, she knew thousands of musicians—and knew exactly which ones she wanted. And with blinding speed and no discernible concern for anyone she might alienate, she'd gone after them, and gotten them.

Now, with the CFSO's premiere less than two weeks away, the music world was watching and waiting for the emergence of a major orchestra—or the downfall of Victoria Paderevsky. Whitney didn't envy her position: The pressures had to be enormous.

She hadn't seen Paddie, as she was known behind her back, in eight years. But eight years ago, during Paddie's tenure at the New York Philharmonic, they had been friends—as much as anyone could be friends with Victoria Paderevsky.

"What a surprise," Whitney said, "but what's this about Harry?"

Paddie huffed. "He's an imbecile, an ingrate. I take it he's not there?"

"No, I haven't heard from him since—I don't know, last week sometime. He calls every week or so. Why?"

Harry Stagliatti was Whitney's teacher and mentor,

and the CFSO's principal horn. Whitney, who fancied she knew him better than anyone else, was still mystified at how Paddie had lured Harry to Florida from his farm in the Adirondacks and a premature retirement. He hadn't bothered to explain, but, as he had packed his bags, had merely said, "I want to see if Florida and *Dr.* Paderevsky are both as godawful as I remember." Like Paddie, Harry was not known for his charm.

"Humph," Paddie said. "Then perhaps he does mean to resign, the scoundrel."

Not knowing what to think, Whitney licked her lips, slightly numb from practicing, and reminded herself that Paddie was also known for her fine-tuned sense of the dramatic. "Victoria, I'm not following you. Are you saying Harry has quit the CFSO?"

"So it would seem," Paddie said tightly.

"But he wouldn't walk out this close to opening night! Where is he? Has he said anything—"

"He left me a letter saying he was going to be away for a couple of days and would miss rehearsal."

"Oh." Whitney relaxed. In Paddie's book, a musician who purposely missed a rehearsal might just as well have chopped off one of her toes. Whitney had always thought tyrannical conductors were martyrs at heart. "Did he say why?"

"No, but I thought you might know."

"I'm sorry, Victoria, but I don't. Something must have come up. He'll be back, I'm sure."

"Not to my orchestra he won't! I will fire him."

"Oh, Victoria." Whitney shook her head, slipping back into the relationship she and Paddie had cultivated eight years ago. Paddie had always tolerated a certain amount of argument—and honesty—from her young friend the horn player. Whitney was never sure why, but thought perhaps it had something to do with the nonjudgmental stance she took toward the controversial conductor. Somehow Whitney's objectivity—it couldn't be called understanding—penetrated Paddie's otherwise thick hide, and something had erupted between them. It wasn't a rapport, and certainly not a close friendship. A tolerance, Whitney thought. An acceptance. She sighed and went on, "You're not going to fire your principal horn this close to your world premiere—and certainly not Harry Stagliatti. He's probably the greatest hornist playing today, and you know it."

"He's missed two and a half days of rehearsal."

"So? That's no reason to fire him. He knows those parts upside down and sideways."

Paddie refused to bend. "And what happens if he doesn't come back? I will have no one to play principal horn."

Whitney could smell a trap. "He'll be back, Victoria. He said so in the letter, didn't he?"

"Yes."

"Then believe it."

There was a short, ominous silence. Then Paddie said in an unusually hushed voice, "I wish I could."

The fire crackled, and Wolfgang yawned. Whitney shivered. It's just the weather, she told herself, and too many years living alone . . . or was there something creepy and foreboding about Paddie's tone? No, she thought, Paddie was just being dramatic. Harry had probably needed a break from what he regularly referred to as "that egotistical tyrant" and had taken a few days off. Who could blame him? But he was also a professional; he would return.

"Whitney," the conductor went on, didactic and under control once again, "you must come to Florida."

"What!"

"I've arranged for you to take the eleven-thirty flight out of New York tomorrow morning. We'll pay your fare, of course."

"Victoria, please, you know I can't—"

"Only you can do *Till* the way Harry does."

Paddie referred to Richard Strauss's *Till Eulenspiegel's Merry Pranks,* which featured a difficult but coveted horn solo and was the opening piece of the CFSO's world premiere. "That's not the point, Victoria," Whitney said lamely. "You can't fire Harry and put me in his place. He's my *teacher.* Imagine what that would do to our relationship."

"But if he doesn't come back, I will need a principal horn—one who can do for this orchestra what Harry could, the cretin. Whitney, you must come."

The presumption of Paddie's tone grated. "I have other commitments."

"I'm only asking for three weeks. Your little orchestra meets once a week. You will miss three rehearsals—no problem. And your wind quintet and brass ensemble don't perform again until late in April. You can come, Whitney. You *must.*"

Leave it to Paddie to do her homework, Whitney thought, but had to acknowledge an unsettling desperation in her words. Victoria Paderevsky was a high-strung woman in a vulnerable position, and Harry Stagliatti's walkout, temporary or not, was a challenge to her authority and a threat to her concentration. It was also, Whitney thought, an incredibly insensitive act on Harry's part. Intensely loyal as she was to him, she knew his faults better than most. And Whitney had been rooting for Paddie for years. They were both women in a man's profession, but, above all, they were musicians. If Whitney could calm Paddie down now by agreeing to fill in for Harry, she owed it to herself and her art at least to try. Chances are, she thought, Harry'll be back by the time I land in Orlando and we can lambast him together, and I can have an all-expenses-paid weekend in the sun.

"What about Harry?" Whitney asked, not willing to give in too easily. "Are you going to fire him?"

She could almost see the conductor's sly smile. "It depends on who plays *Till* better."

"All right, I'll come—but I *won't* replace Harry. When he returns, he gets his seat back and I quit, regardless of what you want to do. Fair enough?"

"Fair enough."

"And, Victoria?"

"Yes?"

"Harry *is* all right, isn't he?"

"I don't know, Whitney."

Dramatics, Whitney thought. "Did you two fight or something?"

"No more so than usual."

"He didn't say why he was leaving?"

"No."

"But he said he would be back?"

"Yes."

Whitney sighed. "Victoria, are you telling me everything? You're sure there isn't something more to this?"

"Just be on that plane tomorrow, Whitney. If Harry hasn't returned by then, perhaps we can come up with a way of finding him."

"Perhaps," Whitney said, and hung up.

Chapter One

THE slush and grayness of March in upstate New York had been replaced by a March so green and beautiful Whitney knew she should have been meandering through Lake Eola Park in downtown Orlando all agog. Instead she was walking with slow but purposeful strides, her horn tucked under one arm, her eyes peering up at a glass high-rise across the street. On the twenty-first floor was the office of the vice president of Graham Citrus, Inc. His name was Daniel Graham, and besides being vice president of a large national citrus corporation and a member of a powerful citrus family, he was chairman of the board of directors of the Central Florida Symphony Orchestra.

And, more to the point, he was the man Victoria Paderevsky suspected had kidnapped Harry Stagliatti.

Yes, Whitney thought wearily, kidnapped. Harry's "couple of days" had now turned into four days, and Paddie had greeted Whitney at the airport with tales of a kidnapped hornist and her dastardly chairman of the board and the Machiavellian politics of her orchestra. Sensing the conductor's growing desperation and paranoia, Whitney had ushered her off to an airport bar and insisted Paddie explain.

"Yesterday you were fairly reasonable," Whitney said, "but today you sound like a raving maniac. What happened?"

Paddie had pursed her lips stubbornly. "I no longer believe Harry left this orchestra of his own free will. I believe he was kidnapped."

"Why?"

"To drive me crazy."

13

Whitney thought it characteristically egotistical of Paddie to think she was at the center of the misfortunes of one of her musicians, but didn't say so. "All right. First, why would anyone think kidnapping Harry would drive you crazy?"

"Not anyone. Only the right person would know that a defection by Harry Stagliatti would upset me more than a defection by any other member of my orchestra. My horn section is my weakest, and yet I have dared to feature it in my opening program. With Harry in first chair, I have every confidence that my gamble will pay off. Without Harry—I don't know."

"And not knowing where Harry is or what he's up to would definitely rock you this close to the premiere. All right, fair enough. I would think someone would try several more standard ways of driving you crazy before resorting to kidnapping French horn players, but—"

"They have been tried," Paddie had said in a near-mumble.

"What? Victoria—"

"I have not wanted to tell you this, Whitney, but I see now that I must confide in someone. Whitney, Harry's disappearance is part of an ongoing plot to drive me from my podium—to make it look as though I cannot handle the pressures of my position. Even before he left, there were episodes. Threatening phone calls—"

"Like what?"

"The usual—leave Florida or pay the consequences, that sort of thing. I tried to ignore them as pranks spawned by jealousy. One morning there was soap in my coffee—or maybe poison, I don't know. I spit it out."

"Did you bring a sample to the police to be tested?"

"No, of course not. I was not injured, and the publicity would only hurt my orchestra. And what if it had only been soap? Who would believe that I had not put it there myself to garner attention? No, I would not risk the police. I still will not. There have been other incidents—a score with the wrong cover, which made me look foolish before my musicians; scores that were hidden so I would seem absentminded to my orchestra and be forced to conduct from memory. And at night at the cottage I have rented there have been noises, lights— Someone is watching me, I'm

sure." Paddie looked at Whitney with her alert, beady
little eyes. "Even now, telling you these things, I can see
how crazy I must sound."

"You're under a great deal of pressure . . ."

"Yes, and these incidents only make matters worse.
They are not extravagances of my imagination, Whitney.
They have happened, and I fear Harry is mixed up in it
somehow."

"But not responsible?"

"That I cannot believe."

Whitney had nodded glumly, sipping her beer. "Why do
you think he's been kidnapped? Just because he's been
gone four days?"

"Four days is too long, yes," Paddie admitted. "But that
is not enough. Whitney, yesterday after talking to you I received another obscene and threatening phone call, and I
began to wonder if maybe something had cracked inside
Harry Stagliatti's cantankerous brain and he *was* behind
all these incidents. So I drove out to the residential hotel
where he was staying. I had already called, of course, but
the desk clerk had said Harry was to be gone for a while
but had retained his rooms. I wondered if perhaps this was
part of his ruse. In any case, I went upstairs, intending to
get into his rooms and search them for clues of where, if
anywhere, he had gone. And do you know what I found?"

Her stomach knotted with tension, Whitney shook her
head. Paddie's sense of drama was getting to her.

"My chairman of the board."

"You're kidding!"

"No," Paddie said gravely. "He did not see me, of course,
but I saw him go into Harry's rooms and I saw him leave,
carrying a sack of Harry's things."

"Oh, Victoria, *no!* You can't think your chairman of the
board is behind this! Why on earth—"

"You haven't met him, Whitney. Daniel Graham is the
kind of man who has always stood in my way. He acts chivalrous and he's terribly handsome, but he does not know
what to do with a strong woman. I threaten men like this.
It is absurd, of course, but it happens."

"Handsome, chivalrous men don't put soap in people's
coffee!"

"Perhaps he didn't do this himself, but he is at the heart of the plot against me."

"Victoria, this is awful. Are you sure—"

"Am I sure I'm not crazy? Hopelessly paranoid?" She smiled, knowing exactly what Whitney was thinking. With her abominable taste in clothes, her excess flesh, her overbite, her thin graying hair, and her deservedly lofty opinion of her skills, Victoria Paderevsky appalled people. She knew it, and didn't care. "No, Whitney," she went on, "I am not crazy or paranoid, although I do admit I have wondered during the past few days if my critics are not right after all. This is absurd, naturally, but, as you say, the pressures on me are tremendous."

"But you enjoy them."

"Yes, I suppose I must."

Whitney had sighed deeply, wondering if Paddie *was* finally falling apart, but refusing to believe it. "This Daniel Graham doesn't sound like the kind of man who would need to go around kidnapping French horn players to get rid of someone he didn't want around. Tell me about him."

Paddie had done her best to give Whitney an overview of CFSO politics and Graham's role in them. Although representative of the growing area's broadening industries and interests, the orchestra's board was dominated by two prominent citrus families, the Grahams and the Walkers. Daniel Graham was chairman of the board and had almost single-handedly secured the majority of financial backing for the risky venture, and his mother, Rebecca Graham, had recommended and fought for the appointment of Victoria Paderevsky as music director. Thomas Walker was a vociferous opponent of Paddie's, and his son, Matthew, was the CFSO's general manager, a soft-spoken proponent of Paddie's, and, to further complicate matters, a friend of Daniel's.

"Why would Daniel Graham want to ruin you?" Whitney had asked finally. "Wouldn't he come out looking bad, too?"

"Not for long, no. People would tend to feel sorry for him and blame me. In the beginning I believed he was on my side, but had to pacify those who oppose me."

"Play both sides against the middle, you mean?"

"Yes. But now I'm afraid he has been converted by my

opposition and believes that I will bring the orchestra to ruin. If he can get rid of me now, before the premiere, then he may still be able to save the orchestra."

"That doesn't make any sense!"

"Yes, it does. If he had gotten rid of me two months ago, the CFSO would have died then and there. But now everything is ready. The orchestra is prepared, the programs are set, the publicity is in place. If I suddenly died or left town, the orchestra *could* conceivably survive. Someone like Daniel Graham would think it could easily survive."

"But where would he find another conductor on such short notice?"

"It can be done."

Whitney had sighed miserably, her doubts slowly being erased by Paddie's calm, rational explanation. "How could anyone believe you'd ruin the CFSO?"

"I am the fat, ugly lady who dares to do music. Who would want to come see my orchestra?"

"Anyone who knows anything about music!"

"Not everyone agrees with you, Whitney."

"But that's disgusting! What difference does it make what you look like or whether you're a man or woman?"

"You know it makes a big difference to far too many people."

"Yes," Whitney said, deflated, "you're right. The question is, what are we going to do about it?"

Paddie's eyes had lit up. "I have a plan."

Now, as she left Lake Eola Park and crossed the busy street, Whitney wondered if perhaps she had been too credible. Looking up at the gleaming high-rise, she wondered why on earth a man like Daniel Graham would go to the extreme of kidnapping a French horn player and making threatening phone calls just to harass Victoria Paderevsky into giving up her podium. He was the vice president of a national citrus corporation, for heaven's sake! Whitney had drunk a glass of Graham premium orange juice that very morning!

It was impossible, she told herself. She was just going along with Paddie's bizarre scheme to pacify her, to calm her frayed nerves. Whatever Harry was up to was perfectly legitimate, if ill-timed, and had simply taken a bit longer than he'd thought. He'd be back. And everything

else was just what Paddie had originally thought it was:
nasty incidents spawned by jealousy.

Yet how did Whitney explain Daniel Graham's visit to
Harry's rooms?

She couldn't, not to her satisfaction.

Besides, there was the chance, however slim, that Paddie was right and Harry had been kidnapped, wasn't
there? And as long as that chance existed, Whitney would
remain cautious and open-minded. She simply couldn't
bear to have anything happen to Harry—or, for that matter, to Paddie.

The revolving doors at the front of the building were still
unlocked. Whitney went through them and smiled at the
security guard. He smiled back. She went straight to the
elevators, banged the UP button, whistled Mozart while
waiting, and walked in when the doors opened up. The
nonstop rise to the twenty-first floor was smooth but fast,
and Whitney's stomach, already not in the best of shape,
flip-flopped several times. She did deep-breathing exercises and, when the doors opened and the bell dinged,
walked out onto the gold-carpeted floor with her stomach
intact.

It was after five, and the reception area was empty.
Whitney fished out the key Paddie had presented her and
walked past two secretarial desks and down a hall to the
last door on the left. Glancing up and down the hall, she
stuck the key in the lock, held her breath, and turned the
key; to her immense surprise and relief, the door opened.

It was a corner office with floor-to-ceiling windows:
quiet, cool, and even more elegant than Whitney had expected. The view of Orlando was stunning. A huge antique
walnut desk stood in front of the windows, and there were
leather chairs and a leather couch, shelves, two nineteenth-century landscape paintings, and an Oriental carpet. There was absolutely no clutter and certainly no
indication whatsoever that the man who occupied this office had kidnapped Harry Stagliatti or poured soap into
Victoria Paderevsky's coffee.

It hardly seemed the man's style, Whitney thought.

"I don't know what you'll find," Paddie had said. "I
don't even know what you should look for, but if you can
find *something* . . . a clue as to his motive, or proof of his

intentions, or an idea of where Harry might be . . . I will be indebted to you, Whitney."

At the time, it had seemed a reasonable proposition. As Paddie had explained, Whitney wasn't really breaking and entering. She had a key, didn't she? (Paddie had shrugged off questions about where she had procured a key to Daniel Graham's office; she was a resourceful woman.)

But now, sensing the power of the man whose office she was about to search, Whitney wondered if she had made a grievous mistake in going along with Paddie. What would happen if she was caught? Guilty or innocent, Daniel Graham wouldn't be pleased. But Paddie had said Daniel Graham was to be at her four o'clock rehearsal, and she would keep him there at all costs. Whitney was safe.

She started with the shelves and worked her way around the room. Everything she touched and examined suggested that Daniel Graham was a wealthy and cultured man . . . and not an especially old one, as Whitney had anticipated. The diploma displayed on one of the shelves, just below the decanters of scotch and bourbon, was only fifteen years old. The man had graduated from the University of Florida the same year Harry had introduced Whitney to the glories of Mozart horn concertos.

She moved to the desk and began rifling through the innocuous drawers, despairing of finding anything incriminating. Clearly, Daniel Graham was the type who would cover his tracks—if he had any to cover. But Paddie would want details, and Whitney was determined to give them to her.

Then, as she was trying to open the bottom right drawer, she heard footsteps out in the hall.

"Just my luck," she muttered to herself, and, not wasting a second in self-recriminations, grabbed her horn and scuttled off to the closet.

With her heart pounding in her chest, she leaped into a dark corner of the closet, which she had already searched, and pulled a herringbone jacket down on top of her, curling up under it and tucking her feet under a tennis racket. The wooden coat hanger made a horrible clanging noise and fell on her head. She was about to toss it aside, but seized it instead, clutching it to her side, listening. If worse came to worse, she wondered, would she be able to beat Daniel Graham over the head with a wooden coat hanger?

The footsteps stopped, and Whitney sat very still, wondering if the oppressive silence was good news or bad news. She was uncomfortable and claustrophobic and furious with Paddie for getting her into this mess and with herself for *letting* Paddie get her into this mess. It was just a janitor, she told herself; nothing to be worried about.

Then the daunting silence exploded. "You might as well come out," a deep, male, and very alert voice said in a distinct drawl. "I assure you, you don't want me to come after you."

Whitney grimaced and held her horn tightly with clammy hands. Breathing the stale, stifling air under the jacket, she acknowledged the dreaded truth: The man beyond the closet door didn't sound at all like a janitor.

"I wouldn't try anything foolish," he said with an annoying air of self-confidence.

Too late for that, Whitney thought dispiritedly. She began to picture herself on a chain gang in some bug-infested swamp. Having waited until age twenty-nine to step foot into Florida, she had her preconceived notions. She pursed her lips and sweated.

"I have a gun," he announced matter-of-factly.

Whitney was not surprised. There was an off chance he was just a security guard doing his job, but she doubted it. He sounded more like Paddie's rendition of Daniel Graham. Probably the gun had been in the locked drawer. And since she had so brilliantly hidden in the closet, Graham had had plenty of time to slip into the drawer and arm himself. From his perspective, she was a possibly dangerous burglar. From her perspective, she was a harmless woman hiding in a closet with a coat hanger and a nickel-plated French horn for protection.

The closet door creaked open, light filtering through the herringbone jacket. Whitney wondered what kind of idiocy had prompted her to hide in a closet. It was a dead end. She breathed through her nose and tried to remain calm, silent, and still. All she needed now was to hyperventilate. She hadn't hyperventilated since high school when she'd played the horn solo in *L'Après Midi d'un Faun.* Nerves. Harry had thrown a paper bag over her head and whacked her on the back. A horn player needed to know how to breathe properly.

So, apparently, did a burglar.

"You will remove the jacket from your face—very slowly."

He spoke in a confident, sonorous drawl, but, of course, he could afford to be confident. He was the one with the gun. It occurred to Whitney that the roles were reversed. *She* was the burglar. *He* was the innocent bystander.

"Need I remind you that I have a gun?"

"You needn't," she replied with as much lighthearted and irreproachable good cheer as she could manage.

Slowly—very slowly—she removed the jacket from her face and wondered what Daniel Graham was making of his dangerous burglar. Once she had agreed to Paddie's scheme, Whitney had disappeared into the women's bathroom at the airport and changed into attire she considered more suitable for breaking into a corporate office: gray sweat pants, a Buffalo Sabres hockey shirt, and pink ballet slippers. She had even tied her ash-brown hair back with a length of thirty-pound fishing line that she had tucked in her horn case. Ordinarily she used the line to string up the complicated valves on her instrument, not to string up her bouncy, dangling curls. She considered herself a strong, sturdy sort of woman—a French horn player had to be— and, with her wide blue eyes, straight nose, and good cheekbones, not unattractive.

She couldn't make out the features of the dark-haired figure in the light of the doorway, but she did see his gun. "I'm not armed," she said in a clear voice. "I know this must look odd, but—"

"Stand up—slowly. We'll talk in a minute."

Whitney was not encouraged. She didn't want to talk. She *couldn't* talk. She had promised Paddie. Not, she thought, that Paddie had kept *her* end of the bargain. She had vowed to keep Daniel Graham at her four o'clock rehearsal, and unless Whitney was very much mistaken, Daniel Graham wasn't at the Orlando Community College auditorium. He was in his office ordering her about with a gun. Brilliant conductor though she might be, Victoria Paderevsky was not a reliable cohort.

"I can't stand up slowly," Whitney said. "I mean, if I do

I'll hit my head on the closet pole and mess up your suits
and—"

"Up."

She shook off the jacket, tucked her horn under one arm,
and leaned forward, at the same time pulling her feet under her so she could get up slowly, without losing her balance. She had a mad urge to catapult herself out of the
corner, but stifled it. The individual giving orders looked
very much as though he would shoot her given sufficient
provocation. Or insufficient provocation.

"What in hell's name have you got—"

He broke off with a growl and grabbed Whitney by the
wrist. She screamed something about lunatics and all this
being a mistake as she and her horn went flying out of the
closet. They landed in a heap on the fringe of an Oriental
carpet. Her horn ended up on the bottom.

"You idiot!" Whitney yelled, prudence gone where her
horn was concerned. "You made me bend my bell!"

But Graham wasn't listening. He pounced on her, pin-
ning her to the floor, and yanked the horn out from under
her. There was a flash of muscled thighs straining against
creased gray linen, and then she was free.

"You maniac!" she groaned into the carpet and rolled
over, sitting up. No wonder Paddie thought him capable of
kidnapping poor Harry!

She shut up at once, regretting her rash comments as
she took in exactly what kind of man she was dealing with.
Clearly he was not an idiot or a maniac. He stood before
her, flourishing her horn in one hand, holding his gun
steadily in the other; tall, intrepid, and solid, just the sort
of aggressive and physical man Whitney had expected
from her search of his office. There was nothing kindly or
gentlemanly about the way he was glaring at her, nothing
restrained and businesslike about his dark, wild hair,
nothing that indicated he was a corporate vice president.
His features were angular, striking, but not pampered,
and their ruggedness suggested he didn't spend all his
time behind a desk. Instead of a suit, he wore casual pants
and a gray gabardine safari shirt. The sleeves were rolled
up, revealing tanned and finely muscled forearms. And yet
there wasn't a single doubt in Whitney's mind that this

was the man whose office she had invaded. This was Daniel Graham.

"What's this?" he demanded, raising her black-encased instrument.

Elbows straightened, palms flat on the wool carpet behind her, Whitney stared up at him. His gun was leveled calmly at her. This isn't happening to me, she thought; it really isn't. If she told him he was brandishing a French horn, he would assume she was connected somehow with the Central Florida Symphony Orchestra, which she was. But he wasn't supposed to know that. If she didn't tell him it was a French horn, he would assume the worst. Once, on a New York subway, a dangerous-looking man had tried to buy her "machine gun" for an ungodly sum. She had finally had to take out her horn and belt out a hunting call before he'd believe it really wasn't a weapon.

"It's nothing," she said lamely. "Just a— *No!* Don't throw it! Please. I think you've already bent my bell. I mean— Oh, blast it all."

The gun didn't move a fraction of an inch; neither did his eyes. They were, Whitney observed in spite of herself, an engaging shade of sea green. She wished his expression was engaging, too, but it wasn't. It was grim and suspicious and not at all reassuring. Paddie had said he was "terribly handsome," hadn't she? Handsome and chivalrous. Only Whitney had yet to see any indication of chivalry.

"All right, all right," she said. "If you must know, it's a bomb. It's set to go off in ten minutes, but you've probably tripped the timer. Why don't we make our exit? You take the stairs; I'll take the elevator."

He gave her an incredulous look, the sea-green eyes narrowing, and turned the case over. On the other side were frayed Tanglewood and Saratoga Performing Arts Center stickers—dead giveaways. "You're a musician," he said. "All right, what's going on? What is this—a horn?"

"Oboe."

"I've seen an oboe case before. This is a French horn."

"Is it?" Whitney shrugged. "I wouldn't know. It's not mine."

"You did say I'd bent your bell, didn't you?" His voice was curiously mild, almost as if he were enjoying himself.

"I don't know, did I? I was in hysterics. Look, I'm un-armed, so would you mind putting your gun away? It's making me nervous."

"I hadn't noticed."

Nevertheless, he laid the gun and her horn on the edge of his desk and folded his arms across his broad chest. With a growing sense of doom, she realized he looked every bit as threatening without his gun as with.

"Well, what are you doing here?" he demanded.

"Visiting. My sister works two floors down. I got lost." She tried not to wince at her own lie. But who would visit her sister in downtown Orlando dressed in sweat pants and pink ballet slippers? Maybe she should have kept on her raw silk suit.

"I see. And you just happen to play French horn and I just happen to be chairman of the CFSO."

Whitney blinked. "Of the what?"

He heaved a sigh and rolled his tongue along the inside of his cheek. If he meant to indicate a certain impatience, he had succeeded, she thought. She could just *see* him dragging Harry off. "The Central Florida Symphony Orchestra. I suppose you're going to tell me you've never heard of it."

"No, of course I've heard of it. But I had no idea you were the—what?"

"Chairman of the board of directors."

"Are you really? My, what a coincidence." Paddie's going to kill me, Whitney thought, unless I kill her first . . . or unless Daniel Graham gets us both. "Look, Mr.—um—"

"Graham," he said, indulging her, but not patiently or with any amusement. "Daniel Graham."

"Oh, well, I guess that stands to reason, this being the offices of Graham Citrus and all." She smiled and went on in her most convincing tone, despite the gnawing uneasiness in the pit of her stomach. "My sister said I could use the ladies' room up here. I guess I lost my way. I'm sorry if I caused you any alarm."

Graham, however, did not appear to be convinced.

"Anyway, Mr. Graham, suppose I just take my horn and go and don't come back?"

He leaned against his desk. "You're not a particularly convincing liar," he said.

I'm not a particularly convincing burglar, either, she thought. "You have a suspicious mind, Mr. Graham."

"Only when I find strange women in my closet. What's your name?"

"Jones. Sara Jones."

"I see. With an *h?*"

"No."

He smiled. "You're improving."

"But you still don't believe me."

"Hardly. How did you get in?"

"Into your closet?" She shrugged, purposely obtuse. She *knew* what he meant. "I just crawled in. I was mindful of the tennis rackets, don't worry."

The muscles in his forearms tightened impressively. "Into my office—how did you get into my office?"

She tried to look both innocuous and reasonable, an elusive combination at best, but, under Graham's intense scrutiny, nearly impossible. "I came through the door," she said. "I thought—I made a wrong turn, Mr. Graham. This is all just a silly mistake."

"Your sister on the nineteenth floor?"

The understated incredulity, the small, wry smile, and the quiet sarcasm did not bolster Whitney's courage, but they were playing on her nerves. Obviously she couldn't tell him the truth, but now she didn't want to. He was enjoying himself far too much. And if he was the kind of man who accosted harmless burglars with a gun, why wouldn't he be the kind of man to kidnap Harry? What if Paddie had been right all along!

"As a matter of fact, yes," she said coolly. "I stumbled into your office while hunting up the ladies' room, and when I heard you coming, I panicked and ducked into the closet. It's as simple as that. Honestly. Just a case of countering one mistake with another. Remember Watergate? Now, if it's all right with you, I'll just apologize and be on my way."

He pushed one foot out in front of the other, bending his knee, his casual, confident stance augmenting his overall air of menacing arrogance. "It's not all right with me," he said blandly.

Whitney pulled her lower lip up over her bottom teeth and bit down hard. She had been afraid it wouldn't be.

"As you know perfectly well," he went on in that quiet, menacing drawl, "my office door was locked."

"Yes," she said, "you're right."

He dropped his hands to his sides and gripped the edge of the desk, the muscles in his powerful arms and legs tensing visibly. The change was small, but perceptible. Daniel Graham was losing patience. "Then how did you get in?" he asked shortly.

"I used a key."

If possible, his look became more threatening.

"You see," she went on blithely, trying to ignore her growing nervousness, "I'm the new custodian."

Graham clenched his teeth and exhaled at the ceiling. "Miss Jones, if you were a cat you'd be well into your ninth life." He dropped his gaze back to her. It was steady now, his eyes a cool and probing green. "And I'm only calling you Miss Jones for the sake of argument. Your name isn't Sara Jones and you're not a custodian. A custodian," he went on more emphatically, "doesn't hide in closets with a damned French horn!"

She had forgotten her horn—momentarily. "It's my dinner break. I practice on my breaks—in an empty office."

"You have an answer for everything, don't you?"

She smiled. "I'm just trying to sort this out—"

"—to your advantage."

"Self-preservation runs high and strong in my bones," she said cheerfully. "May I go now?"

"Miss Jones," he said, sitting on the edge of the desk, "the building custodians do not have the key to this office."

"They don't?"

"No."

She looked him straight in the eye and said, "Then how did I get in?"

"A key," he said, "which you will give me before we leave—along with an explanation of where you got it and what you're doing here. I have a feeling I'm not going to like what I hear, but I'll be damned if— *What do you think you're doing?*"

Whitney didn't take the time to answer. She was on her

feet and gone—through the door, past the reception area, to the elevators. It had been Paddie's idea to break in after five—Paddie's ideas, Paddie's keys, Paddie's suspicions. Whitney's hide. She banged the DOWN button, realized there wasn't time to wait, and hunted for the stairs.

She saw the red exit sign down the hall and ran.

Chapter Two

DANIEL GRAHAM intercepted her at the door, blocking her escape with his big body. "We're not finished," he said calmly.

"I have nothing more to say," Whitney declared, gulping for air. Her gasping had more to do with terror than aerobic fitness. "Call the police, if you insist!"

"All right."

That took the wind right out of her sails. He was willing to call the police? While she stood there dumbfounded, he caught her by the elbow and escorted her back to his office. He was at least half a foot taller than her five-five. She didn't know why she noticed, but she did. She didn't know why her eyes kept wandering up to his face as he marched her along, but they did. There was a sexual magnetism about the man that she found quite impossible to ignore. Perhaps it was adrenaline, or the brush of his thigh on her hip, or just exhaustion. He was an arrogantly masculine man, and ordinarily Whitney wouldn't have found him the least bit attractive.

Florida, she decided, was doing strange things to her mind and body.

Graham urged her into his office and kicked the door shut behind him. She observed the dark hairs on the wrist clamped around her forearm and the way the muscles tightened as he sat her down in a leather chair. He released her, and she leaned back, unable to suppress a yawn.

"Jesus," he said.

"It's been a long day," Whitney replied.

He pointed a finger at her and told her to stay put. Then

he went around and stood behind the desk. "You're Victoria Paderevsky's new horn player, aren't you?"

"No."

"You're not supposed to arrive until tomorrow. I had no idea she'd hired a woman, but then one never knows about our Dr. Paderevsky. Do you know her?"

"Victoria Pader—" She fumbled at the last syllables.

"Paderevsky," Graham supplied.

"We've never met."

"You're lying, Miss Jones."

"Why don't you ask her, then?"

Whitney was confident Paddie would deny her.

"I intend to," Graham said, lifting the phone. At least Whitney assumed it was a telephone. The contraption looked as though it could run Graham Citrus in the absence of any and all of its many employees. Possibly it did. Suddenly he banged the receiver back down. "She sent you here, didn't she? I'll be damned. What does that wretched woman think I've done now? I suppose she blames me for Harry Stagliatti cutting out on her?"

"Harry Stagliatti?" Whitney said blankly. It wasn't a good effort; she'd known Harry far too long. She smiled vapidly, no easy task since she was anything but. "I'm sorry, Mr. Graham, I don't know what you're talking about."

"I didn't think you would," he said dryly. "But if you're a horn player, you've heard of Harry Stagliatti, and I have a feeling that—" He broke off with a growl. "Curse that woman!" Then he picked up the phone again.

"What are you doing?"

"Calling the police." He punched a button. "Sorry, sweets, but your wide-eyed innocent act hasn't worked. If you won't explain to me, you can explain to the police."

She didn't realize she had been doing a wide-eyed innocent act. "Suppose we make a deal—"

"No deals." He punched two more buttons.

"All right." She licked her lips and considered her plight. The police would come and arrest her for breaking and entering. She would have to tell them she was Whitney McCallie, new principal horn for the CFSO. Paddie would be called. Paddie would claim ignorance. Whitney would go to jail. It was, she thought, an unpleasant scenario. Could she persuade Paddie to go public about the nasty incidents that had occurred the past few days and her own suspicions? It was unlikely. And Graham's willingness to call in the police might be enough to prove to Paddie he was innocent, in which case Whitney herself wouldn't want Paddie to go public. They would both come out looking like fools.

"All right," she repeated gravely, as though deciding, finally, to tell the truth, which, of course, was out of the question. She looked up at Graham and smiled, ignoring his glower. At least he'd stopped punching buttons. "I don't have a sister on the nineteenth floor and I'm not a custodian. I'm a horn player. I know all about Harry Stagliatti and his resignation from the CFSO. I figured maybe this was my chance. There's a vacancy in the CFSO horn section, and I wanted to fill it. I came here hoping to compel you to intervene on my behalf—you know, cut through the orchestral bureaucracy's red tape. There's an enormous prejudice against female horn players, you know."

"I can't imagine why," Graham said sardonically. "How was I supposed to help?"

She shrugged. "I thought you might have a few ideas of your own."

She regretted her comment at once and felt a flush coming on, but Graham, she observed with some relief, was a single-minded individual. He gave her a hard, disbelieving look. "And how was hiding in my closet supposed to persuade me to help you?"

"It wasn't," she said quickly. "I chickened out when I heard you coming, and hid."

Graham burst out laughing.

She started to glare up at him, but consciously altered her look to a gaze of ingenuous surprise. But even as she concentrated on her act and suppressed her irritation, she couldn't fail to notice that he had a glorious laugh. How could a man with such a deep, rich laugh possibly have kidnapped Harry Stagliatti and done all those nasty and peculiar things to Paddie? Not that Graham wasn't capable of surefooted action when the situation required it—hence her being hauled out of his closet at gunpoint and so forth—but that his approach would be much more direct and immediately productive.

"A femme fatale you are not," he said, his laughter fading. "A seductress doesn't wear pink ballet slippers and carry around a goddamned French horn. You may be cute, but that's about it. Sorry, dear heart, but your lie isn't working—and my patience has run out."

Cute! She jumped to her feet, but Graham slammed down the receiver, picked it up again, and began punching a fresh set of buttons. "Wait—"

"No more. You've had your chance."

"Don't call the police. I haven't stolen anything. I—"

"I'm not calling the police. I've changed my mind. I'm calling Victoria Paderevsky. The three of us are going to have a little chat."

That was even worse! Paddie would *never* understand, and Graham would have them both at his mercy—before they could consult and work out a story to their mutual advantage. Whitney silently cursed Paddie for talking her into this bit of skulduggery. "Look," she said in desperation, rising, "this isn't what you think it is—"

"Isn't it? Look, Dr. Paderevsky and I have had our differences, but I'll be damned if I'm going to stand around and let her send musicians out to burglarize my office! She's going to explain—and so are you."

Whitney chewed miserably on her lower lip and debated ways she could regain control of the situation. Paddie and Graham and Whitney's own easygoing nature had put her between the proverbial rock and hard place. What was she supposed to do now? Save my own skin, she thought, and Paddie's, if I can. She smiled weakly at Graham, but he wasn't paying attention. He had the phone to his ear and was turned sideways, glancing out the floor-to-ceiling window behind him. Twenty-one stories below, Orlando glistened in the Florida sun.

Surreptitiously, Whitney took a step toward the desk. He didn't notice. She refused to think. Without considering the consequences, she lunged at the desk, grabbed the gun first, then her horn, and ran.

"*Damn it, woman, come back here!*"

Whitney ignored the angry bellow. This time she knew where she was going—*and* she had the gun. She hoped only that Graham believed she would use it, which she wouldn't—and that she wouldn't trip and shoot herself in the foot. Explaining to Paddie was going to be hard enough as it was.

"We've blown it," Whitney said with feeling.

"Yes," Victoria Paderevsky replied gravely. "I'm afraid we may have only made matters worse."

They were sitting on the deck of Paddie's cottage drinking gin-and-tonics and bemoaning their fate. The cottage, of uninsulated clapboards painted a cheerful yellow, was set amid a grove of blossoming citrus trees with a scent like heaven. There wasn't any yard to speak of, but the deck stretched out across the front of the cottage and was shaded on one end by a pink dogwood. Whitney had wondered if Paddie had finally gone off the deep end when she'd turned off the highway onto a narrow, sandy road that cut straight through a grove of late-ripening Valencia oranges and to the cottage. Leave it to Paddie, Whitney had thought, to find herself a peaceful retreat.

"I'm glad you said 'we,'" Whitney muttered.

"Yes, but of course you know that I cannot get involved. Daniel Graham mustn't find out I put you up to this escapade today."

"I agree. He'll think you're a fruitcake for sure. Look, obviously Graham has his suspicions, but I don't see why they have to lead to you. He'll find out I'm Harry's student and figure I acted on my own. I'm sure he'll interrogate you"—Daniel Graham did not merely ask questions; he interrogated—"but you can claim you didn't know anything at all about my harebrained scheme."

Paddie raised her thick brows. "Are you implying my plan was faulty?"

"That's a moot point. What you claim and what he thinks are all that matter now."

"What about you?"

"I'll muddle through."

That was good enough for Paddie. It never occurred to her that Whitney was going to extraordinary lengths to protect her, but, then, Whitney knew it wouldn't. "If he followed you and saw us meeting, he'll know he was right and there is a connection between us."

"He didn't see us, Victoria. I'm sure he tried to follow me, but he had to be careful. I had his gun, don't forget, and he couldn't possibly know if I'd use it."

"Would you have?"

Whitney sighed in despair. Only Paddie would ask. "Of course not!"

"Not even to save me?"

"Victoria, please. *You* were never in any danger."

Whitney had already gone over every detail of her narrow escape from the clutches of Daniel Graham, which had included racing down twenty-one flights of stairs, hiding in a supply closet, and venturing out into the unfamiliar streets of Orlando trying to look normal in sweat pants and ballet slippers and carrying a French horn. At least she had had the wherewithal to slip the gun in with the horn during her sojourn in the supply closet. She'd taken a taxi to her rendezvous with Paddie at the Haagen-Dazs stand at the Fashion Square Mall, but Paddie was an hour late. Railing about the "idiots" she was conducting, she'd bundled Whitney off to the airport to pick up the rest of her luggage.

Paddie started to lecture her on the stupidity of having taken her horn with her just because she didn't want to trust it to an airport locker, but Whitney didn't let her get far. For the first time in her life, she blew up at a conductor. In no uncertain terms, she told Paddie that if she had done *her* part, Daniel Graham never would have seen Whitney and her horn.

"Graham should have been with you," she shrieked, "not pointing a gun at me!"

And Paddie had calmly replied, "Even I cannot will a man into my presence. He told me he would attend my rehearsal. If he had, I would have kept him there. He did not."

"You could have cut your rehearsal short and done something to warn me!"

"We were working on the Stravinsky," Paddie had said, as if that explained—and excused—everything.

Whitney had wanted to take the next available flight back to New York, but she simply couldn't. Harry Stagliatti hadn't shown up for the four o'clock rehearsal, either. He had been gone a full four days without a word to anyone, even Whitney. And now she, too, was worried. *Was* his disappearance part of a plot to drive Paddie from her podium? *Was* Daniel Graham involved? Whitney had questions, but no answers. There was only one certainty: Victoria Paderevsky would rather be assassinated on the podium than resign her post as music director of the Central Florida Symphony Orchestra. She had worked too hard and alienated too many people to leave voluntarily or to let anyone try to force her into collapsing under the strain of her position. Nothing short of murder or being fired would keep her off the podium on opening night.

"Daniel Graham is a dangerous man," Paddie said, not for the first time.

"Maybe so, but I can think of lots of other people who would want to ruin you more than he would," Whitney said bluntly—and truthfully.

"Name five."

"I can name a hundred—and so can you."

"No one likes me."

"Which is no one's doing but your own. *You* don't like anyone, Victoria."

Paddie drained the last of her gin-and-tonic and pursed her fleshy lips. "This business is affecting my work."

"I know," Whitney said softly.

On the surface, Paddie seemed just as irascible and efficient as ever, but Harry's inexplicable disappearance and the subtle, nasty incidents of harassment had to be taking their toll. But Whitney wouldn't know for sure if Paddie was holding up until she saw her conduct. Only then could anyone count on seeing the real Victoria Paderevsky.

"We must get to the bottom of this," Paddie said.

"Perhaps we should go to the police—"

"Impossible. I have no evidence. Come, Whitney, what would they say? The pressures have finally gotten to the fat lady; she is cracking. No, I must have proof."

"You're a brilliant conductor. They'd listen to you."

"Phooey. I'm the fat lady they do not understand."

Whitney knew Paddie wasn't feeling sorry for herself. She was simply stating the facts as she knew them. What other people thought of her had never had any bearing whatsoever on her own opinions of her gifts. "They could ask Daniel Graham what he was doing at Harry's hotel."

"You don't understand the Graham family's position in this community. Even if the police did go so far as to ask him for an explanation—and this would be a miracle—they would believe anything he says. And if he *has* kidnapped Harry . . ."

Whitney shook her head, thinking of the capable and direct man she had dealt with that afternoon. "I just can't see it, Victoria. I know he isn't the most charming man in the world, but kidnapping Harry to drive you crazy? It just doesn't fit."

"Suppose Harry had found out Graham was harassing me?"

"Then that's a different story," Whitney said heavily. "He'd have to shut him up and— Oh, Victoria, I can't stand not knowing!"

"Yes, but we must be cautious. If we go to the police precipitously, we could make things worse for Harry. And if I am wrong or right, the publicity will hurt the orchestra— and what would happen to you? Daniel Graham would squash you like a tiny little black ant."

"He still might."

"Yes."

"You don't have to agree, you know."

"But I must speak my mind. Whitney, this Graham is a powerful man in central Florida. Graham Citrus owns thousands and thousands of acres throughout the state. No matter how justifiable and noble your motives, you did break into his office."

"At your bidding, Victoria."

Paddie sat back and folded her hands on her ample middle. "Where's your proof?"

"You'd deny me!" It was not a question, but an exclamation of an unpleasant but not unexpected fact. Whitney sighed. "All right, then, now what?"

"We wait for Graham to make his next move."

"I could end up on a chain gang in some swamp."

"That's possible."

"You're a big help. Do you think he'll come here looking for me?"

"Undoubtedly. If you had not brought your horn—"

"Let's not start that again," Whitney snapped.

"Yes, what's done is done," Paddie said philosophically.

"Graham suspects who you really are and suspects my involvement. We must convince him you acted alone. He will want to talk to me, of course, which means you can't stay here."

"Why not? If he comes around, I'll just hide. He won't search your closets—"

Paddie was shaking her head. "No, impossible."

"Victoria, this is no time to protect your privacy. Everyone in the music world knows you prefer to live in seclusion, but if someone's trying to ruin you, you should let me stay here with you and run interference. I can intercept the obscene phone calls and—"

Paddie was still shaking her head.

"All right, all right. Where do I stay, then? You *have* made other arrangements?"

"No."

"Terrific."

"Whitney, Whitney, I have been unable to think clearly. I myself would find elsewhere to stay, but I am afraid to do anything suspicious."

Whitney snorted in disbelief. Paddie was using her fake Lithuanian accent, which meant she was either lying or expostulating. In this case, lying. Thus far, Paddie had greeted all her bizarre happenings with irritation and contempt, but not fear—at least not overtly. Underneath, Whitney sensed a certain desperation in Paddie's actions. But, on the surface, as far as Paddie was concerned, the entire business was nothing more than a nuisance. *She* hadn't felt Daniel Graham's iron-hard grip or looked into his sea-green eyes—

Whitney caught herself: What did Graham's sea-green eyes have to do with anything?

She got Paddie's point, however: She couldn't stay at the cottage. She threw up her hands in half-mock, half-real despair. "So here I am in Florida during the peak tourist season—at nine o'clock at night, no less—with no place to stay. *And* I'm exhausted. Some thanks I get for risking my life with a lunatic."

"What about your friends in the orchestra?"

"They'd be even less likely than you to cover for me if Graham came around asking questions and suggesting I was a thief—and they don't know I'm in Florida, remember? No one expects me until tomorrow."

Paddie nodded thoughtfully. "Yes," she said, "and perhaps it is best that they don't find out. To explain to them would cause unnecessary strain and gossip. Already I am dissatisfied with their progress, especially with the Stravinsky."

She said *Straveensky*. Expostulating. But Whitney knew better than to suggest her life and freedom ought to be more important than the Central Florida Symphony Orchestra's premiere performance of *The Firebird Suite*. Whitney felt like a fugitive with nowhere to run.

"I have a tent," Paddie was saying.

Whitney couldn't stop her jaw from dropping. "You're not serious."

"It's in the storage closet. It was here when I arrived. I believe it's old, but I'm sure it's still serviceable."

"You expect me to sleep in a tent? Victoria, I haven't slept since dawn!"

"I have a blanket."

"How generous. And where am I supposed to pitch my tent?"

"In the grove, here. You'll be safe. It's a large grove—two thousand acres." Paddie hesitated, as if about to say something else, but changed her mind. She smiled. "I'm sure there's a charming spot to camp. And tomorrow you can find a place to stay."

Not "we," Whitney noticed, but "you." She swore under her breath, but Paddie was already lifting her bulk off her wooden chair. "What about food?" Whitney asked, trailing after the conductor into the cottage.

"I'll give you some to take with you—no, that might attract animals."

"Victoria!"

Whitney argued and cajoled, but Paddie was convinced she'd arrived at the perfect solution. She would leave food on the deck, and Whitney could sneak up in the morning and get it, like a raccoon. Whitney watched, amazed, while Paddie dug happily in the closet until she came up with an army green, foul-smelling pup tent. "See," she said, thrusting the thing at Whitney, "all the stakes are here. If

I was smaller and younger, I would leap at the chance to camp out in this beautiful weather."

Since Whitney was both smaller and younger, she supposed she should leap. But somehow she couldn't. Instead, she resignedly stretched out her arms and let Paddie pile on the mildewy tent and a flannel blanket that smelled of mothballs, then stood there shaking her head while Paddie trudged off to the bedroom for a pillow.

"Arghhh! That son of a toad!"

Whitney dropped the tent and ran. Paddie was letting loose with a string of unladylike but appropriate expletives and holding a sheet of orange construction paper in one large hand. Peering over her shoulder, Whitney saw the source of Paddie's fury. It was a drawing, done in black ink. In the middle of the page was a caricature even more unflattering than the real Victoria Paderevsky. Gathered around the unhappy figure, pointing their fingers, smirking, laughing, were a dozen of the famous established conductors of the world.

"There's your proof, Victoria," Whitney said softly, her stomach twisted.

Paddie drew in a deep breath. "Do you think I would show this to anyone?" she demanded hoarsely. "Laugh at the fat lady, all! Come, laugh! See how she jiggles! The fat lady who dares to do music. *No!*"

"Victoria—"

She crumpled up the horrible drawing. Her tiny eyes were shining with determination, and, for an instant, Whitney thought she saw the hurt. "I will not be cowed. I will not be ruined. I will fight. I will do music! You must help me, Whitney. Help me."

Chapter Three

WHITNEY decided to pitch her tent between two stately old citrus trees on the edge of a narrow, sandy road. Paddie had warned Whitney away from the small lake behind her cottage: The owner of the groves lived on the other side and there was no point in pushing her luck by camping out too close to the main house. Whitney had quite agreed, but the groves were immense, divided by a confusing web of paths and roads, and she wasn't sure exactly where she was. So she just dropped her things and hoped for the best. If the crocodiles didn't get her, she figured the snakes and the fire ants would.

That would be a delightful obituary, she thought, pounding in the final stake with a crumbling brick. Naturally Paddie hadn't offered to help carry anything. Once she had gotten over the shock of finding the drawing, she had cheerfully arranged the tent, a flashlight, blanket, horn, leather satchel, canvas bag, and suitcase in Whitney's outstretched arms, hooking things on her fingers and shoulders, assuring her she'd be just fine out there in the Florida wilderness. Twice on her journey Whitney had dropped everything.

After pitching the tent, she collapsed onto a bed of clover and wild flowers, having checked first for snakes and ant nests. She leaned against her suitcase and sighed at the clear night sky. The full moon cast eerie shadows and gave a silvery tint to the sandy road and the citrus blossoms— great white flowers glowing against the dark, waxy leaves. Whitney had no idea if she was parked under a grapefruit or an orange tree, but supposed it didn't matter. She sighed, tired but keyed up.

Was Harry out here somewhere, buried under an orange tree, held prisoner in a snake pit? Whitney shuddered and checked her thoughts. She noticed every sound and every movement in the still, warm, sweet-scented night.

And remembered the noises and lights Paddie had thought were a part of the plot against her . . .

No, Whitney thought, I must be a mile from the cottage. . . . I won't get the creeps.

Finally, she got out her horn and played a few soft warm-ups. Whole notes, mostly, in the lower two octaves of the horn's four-octave range. Peaceful sounds. Her mind wandered. She thought of Harry. He loathed almost as many people as Paddie did. But, unlike Paddie, people liked him. He was portly, bald, brilliant, and irreverent— but he was a virtuoso horn player, not a conductor, and he was a man in a man's profession, not a woman.

But was he in danger?

Whitney started down the scale slowly, still playing softly in whole notes, glad that Daniel Graham hadn't done any permanent damage to her horn. The drawing had changed everything. That wasn't Paddie's imagination. But could Graham possibly be responsible? She recalled how he'd laughed and commented on her ballet slippers and sweat pants . . . and her cuteness.

And quite calmly, in the lovely night air, she admitted to herself that she didn't want him to be responsible for any of the goings-on at the CFSO.

Perhaps she should simply have told him the truth?

She started down the scale, slowly, patiently. The acoustics in the grove were terrible. The sound was just lost into the night. Whitney didn't mind. It felt good to practice.

Something rustled behind the tent, on the other side of the road. Or was it off to her left? Whitney halted the stream of air into her horn and sat very still, the mouthpiece still pressed to her lips. Her embouchure relaxed while the rest of her tensed.

Did crocodiles wander through citrus groves at night? Maybe there was a swamp nearby—

A twig snapped.

A snake?

Lizards?

Harry?

Whitney reached into her canvas bag and rummaged around for the cold, hard feel of Daniel Graham's gun.

"I wouldn't if I were you," his voice said from the shadows.

Her fingers curled around the butt of the revolver, but she froze. If nothing else, she was too shocked to move. How had he found her? Surely Paddie hadn't told him!

Daniel Graham stepped out from the shadows and stood two paces in front of her. He looked just as tall and intrepid outdoors as he had in, only this time he had a rifle pointed at her.

"I might have known it was you," he said. "Were you playing that thing?"

"My horn? Yes, I—"

"It sounded like a dying cow."

"How nice."

"Remove your hand from the bag, Ms. McCallie. Slowly. And it had better come out empty."

Her eyes widened. "My name—"

"Your hand," he said, and prompted her with his rifle.

She let go of the gun and lifted her hand slowly from the bag. "I was just going after my spit rag," she said lamely.

Graham grunted, swooped down, grabbed the bag, and pulled out the gun. He gave her a cold look. She shrugged her shoulders and observed he had changed into jeans and a work shirt, the sleeves, again, rolled up to his elbows. His hair was wild and dark, windblown in the warm night. She found herself wishing he didn't have the rifle, wishing he hadn't taken things from Harry's room, wishing she could stop the grind of suspicion and tell him everything.

"All right," she said. "So I thought you were a crocodile."

"There aren't any crocodiles in Florida."

"Oh. Well. Whew. What a relief. I'll get blown to pieces instead of eaten alive."

He scowled down at her. "How the hell can you be sarcastic when you have two guns pointed at you?"

"Would you rather I weep and plead?"

"As a matter of fact, yes."

He tucked the revolver in his waistband and cradled the rifle in his arms, studying her. She hadn't bothered to change out of her sweat pants, and she'd torn the fishing line out of her hair during her wait for Paddie. Now it just tumbled over her shoulders however it pleased. She longed for a bath. Daniel Graham looked so fresh and clean and damnably in control. Probably he'd gone home and had a nice hot shower and a tall, cool drink. Several, undoubtedly. Whitney thought of her cozy home and Wolfgang and her fireplace. What she wouldn't give for them now!

She wasn't at all sure what he meant to do—or how he knew her name and had found her. Or why she wasn't particularly afraid. Because he hadn't slaughtered her back in Orlando when he'd had the chance? That didn't make any sense. But, then, not much had so far.

Since he was armed and she wasn't, she decided to let him call the shots. So to speak, she thought with a slight choke.

"Hell," he growled.

"Are you going to take me to the police?" she asked. "I'll go quietly. Here, let me put my horn away."

"Don't move."

Whitney didn't move.

Graham frowned down at her, the moonlight casting shadows on his angular features, augmenting—quite unnecessarily, Whitney thought—his menacing look. "I won't be calling the police," he said ominously. "This is just between us, Ms. McCallie."

"Somehow that doesn't reassure me, Mr. Graham," she replied.

He grinned sardonically. "I didn't think it would. You put up a hell of a chase this afternoon."

"It's all those sixteenth notes and triple-tonguings I do."

"I'm sure," he said wryly.

"I don't get winded easily."

The barest hint of a smile touched his all too memorable mouth. "No?"

She didn't like his tone. It was too intimate, too seductive, for a man with a rifle. "No," she repeated with finality and decided she would be better off not trying to explain diaphragmatic breathing and such to him. The man obviously didn't understand musicians. "You know, you don't need all those weapons. I'll cooperate. Do you always carry a gun?"

"No, but there's been trouble with poachers in the area.

However, if I'd known I'd be dealing with you, I'd have brought along a few more weapons. I've underestimated you once today. I don't intend to make the same mistake twice."

"You didn't underestimate me." She did *not* want to wound this man's male ego, at least not as long as he had the rifle and she just had her French horn. "I was just protecting myself. You caught me at an awkward moment. Now, of course, everything's changed."

"It has, has it?" He seemed incredulous, wryly amused, and totally confident. And tall, Whitney thought; very tall.

Intending to look nonchalant, she leaned back against her suitcase and kicked out her feet, her horn lying across her thighs. "I'm not in your office," she pointed out. "And you have no proof that I ever was there. There's nothing you can do to me, and therefore no reason for me to run."

"I can nail you for trespassing, Ms. McCallie."

She tugged the small mouthpiece off her horn. "Ah, but you're trespassing, too," she said, almost idly, as she dumped her spit that had accumulated in the tangled tubing of her horn into the grass. "We'd both go down together, Mr. Graham."

He laughed once, curtly. "And I thought you'd given up on the wide-eyed innocent act. This is my land, Ms. McCallie. Don't pretend—"

"Your land!"

Unable to stop herself, Whitney leaped to her feet, horn dangling from one hand, ready to accost Daniel Graham. He was lying. He had to be! Paddie would have told her this was his land! Even she wasn't that crazy!

Graham shifted the rifle, just enough to remind Whitney of its presence. "Easy," he warned.

She caught her breath and sat back down. "You're not serious," she said, but she knew he was.

Paddie had deliberately not told Whitney that the groves belonged to Daniel Graham. No wonder she had warned Whitney away from the main house! Damn her, Whitney thought. From Paddie's point of view, it all made perfect sense. If Whitney had known this was Graham property, she would have insisted on staying at the cottage. And even if she had by some weird chance let Paddie talk her into camping out on his land anyway, Whitney would have had to *pretend* ignorance. Now her ignorance was real.

"So you are going to pretend you didn't know you're camping in my grove," Graham said.

"But I didn't."

"You fail to amuse me, Ms. McCallie."

"So I've gathered. Look, can't we be friends?"

He eyed her for a moment. The shadows hid his eyes, but she could see his wariness and suspicion in the hard line of his jaw. "I think you should explain," he told her in an altogether steely drawl.

"I did—this afternoon, remember? About the male-dominated orchestral bureaucracy and—"

"Enough! I don't know what your game is, but, damn it, I'm going to find out. Dr. Paderevsky was mysteriously unavailable this evening, but I spoke to Bradley Fredericks and Yoshifumi Kamii. Do you know who they are?"

"No." She was lying, of course.

"Poor Whitney, always the last to know anything." He didn't sound particularly sympathetic. Or credulous. "Bradley is the associate conductor and principal violist of the CFSO. Yoshifumi is the concertmaster. They told me a twenty-nine-year-old female horn player was due to arrive tomorrow to take Harry Stagliatti's place. Dr. Paderevsky hired her. She's from Schenectady, New York, and her name is Whitney McCallie."

"Me?"

"You."

Whitney sagged. "Betrayed at every turn."

Graham ignored her. "This Whitney McCallie, according to Bradley and Yoshifumi both, is hornist with the Empire State Wind Quintet out of New York City and the Capital District Brass Ensemble out of Albany. She also is the conductor of the Mohawk Valley Community Orchestra. Two months ago she was offered a position with the Cleveland Symphony Orchestra, but refused."

"Fourth horn," she said. "I'm not as good in the lower octaves. And I'm not your basic Cleveland type."

"But you *have* penetrated the 'male-dominated orchestral bureaucracy,' haven't you?" He paused to smile with a certain, measured irony. Then, abruptly, he was serious once more. "Yoshifumi intimated that in another five years you'd be one of the strongest, most innovative hornists in the country—something to do with your tone."

"How nice of Yoshifumi."

Knowing Yoshifumi as she did, Whitney suspected he had realized she'd already managed to get herself on Graham's black list and was trying to protect her.

"My horn teacher says when I play my tone is so round he can see the oranges falling out of my bell," she went on glumly. There was no point in worsening her position by telling him Harry Stagliatti was her horn teacher.

Graham looked at her sternly, the shadows dancing on his face. His jeans, she noticed unwillingly, fit snugly over his thighs. The man was in incredible physical shape—probably from stalking burglars and trespassers. "Then you're admitting you're Whitney McCallie?" he said icily.

"Sure, why not? Seems to me my ship is sinking."

"Seems to me your ship has sunk." He smiled suddenly, visibly relaxing now that she had begun, in however small a way, to cooperate. "No more lies, all right? I want to know why you were in my office this afternoon. I realize we didn't meet under the best of circumstances, but I still think you ought to tell me."

"Or?"

"Or nothing. I just need to know."

Whitney sighed. It was an appealing argument—simple and direct. And somehow it was more effective than his guns and dark looks. She was inclined to take the chance and tell him the truth. Possibly he had a perfectly innocent explanation for being in Harry's hotel room. But the truth wasn't an option. There was still Paddie to consider, and Harry.

She popped her mouthpiece back on her horn and grinned up at him. "I'm in love with you," she said lightly. "I saw your picture in some publicity on the orchestra and those clear sea-green eyes of yours and thought to myself—"

"All my publicity photos are in black and white."

"Yes, but I *knew* you had sea-green eyes."

"Give up, Whitney," he said, but the use of her first name and the flash of his smile told her she'd penetrated his somber mood. "Or maybe *I* should give up. You aren't going to tell me what you were doing in my office, are you?"

"I'm not at liberty to."

"All right, then. I have a fair idea, anyway. Harry Stagliatti, right?"

Whitney felt her throat go dry, but she managed to lift her shoulders in an idle shrug. "All I know is that Stagliatti walked out on Dr. Paderevsky and I have to fill his shoes—no easy task, I assure you. He's a magnificent hornist."

"Yes," Graham ground out. *"Damn.* Look, I'm not going to spend the entire night arguing with you. I want the key you used to get into my office. Give it to me and I'll go."

"The key? Oh, you believed me!" She laughed and hoped she was the only one who could hear how hollowly. "No, no, I don't have a key. I bribed a janitor."

"Damn it, woman!" he hissed angrily, but quickly reined in his temper. "Only I have a key to my office."

"Then how could I have one?"

He slung his rifle over his shoulder and took one long step toward her. His toes were just inches from hers. It was all she could do to stop herself from snatching her feet away, shriveling them up like the Wicked Witch of the East. Her heart beat wildly. Had she pushed him too far? What if he had come out into the grove to check on Harry in the snake pit and had stumbled on her? Or maybe he was on his way to Paddie's cottage to make her think someone was watching her? Poachers, indeed. Who would steal grapefruit blossoms?

Graham gave her just enough time to panic before he asked calmly, "Would you like me to search your belongings until I find it?"

Whitney reached over and dug around in her decrepit canvas bag. There was a bust of Beethoven silkscreened on the outside. If Graham noticed, he said nothing. She suddenly realized the man was skulking about in his grove without a flashlight. The moon was bright, but, in her estimation, not that bright. She withdrew a deerskin chamois cloth and glanced around at him. He had his rifle pointed at her. "That's not necessary," she said crisply. "I'm not likely to attack you with anything less than a machine gun—"

"The key, please."

She unfolded the rag and, trying to ignore the long barrel of the rifle, handed over his accursed key. "Enjoy," she said.

"This had better be your only copy."

It wasn't. Paddie would never have let Whitney use her only copy of such an important weapon. "Of course. Why would I need two?"

"If I catch you in my office again, I'm going to drag you to the police by your heels. Is that understood?"

"Perfectly."

"And I'm not in any mood to rescue you from a band of poachers. You'd better be off my property by noon tomorrow."

"Gladly."

He moved in front of her, so that they were again toe-to-toe and she could see the muscles tensed in his arms and the hard set of his jaw. His shadow cast over her. With one finger, he tilted her chin up toward him. But, surprisingly, when he spoke, his drawl was sonorous and almost gentle. "And Whitney," he said, "stick to playing your damned horn."

She thought he would turn on his heels and disappear into the night, but he didn't. He cupped her elbows and brought her to her feet. Her horn was between them, but he didn't notice, and neither did she. She only noticed his eyes. They were a cool, cool green, and yet they seemed to burn with bridled passion and intensity. They were eyes she could look at for a long time.

He smiled, and up close it was more powerful, more sensual, than ever. "I don't think I've ever wanted to kiss a woman in sweat pants as much as I do you," he said in a low, lazy drawl. "Why do you think that is, Whitney?"

"Maybe it's my French horn . . ."

"Maybe it's you."

And finally he did kiss her, his mouth lightly grazing her lips. He touched her cheek, his skin as cool as the night air. Whitney gripped her horn, but was too mesmerized by the play of his lips and tongue on her mouth to pull back. Harry would say she was jumping out of the frying pan into the fire. She would agree, and jump willingly. She could seem to do nothing else.

"Noon," he said, and was gone before she had finished her nod.

Not only did the tent stink, but it leaked. Having seen the holes and handled the worn fabric, Whitney was not surprised. What surprised her was the rain. Not long after Graham left, her beautiful starlit sky gave way to monstrous dark clouds, and the rain came in great gushing torrents. In disbelief, she crammed her belongings into the tent and wrapped herself in Paddie's blanket, swatting mosquitoes and cursing the Sun Belt. The old canvas began dripping almost immediately. She might as well have pitched a sheet.

Waving around the thin beam of the flashlight, she contemplated her dilemma. She could stay here and be washed into a swamp and be devoured by alligators or captured by poachers, or she could venture out into the grove and find shelter. Paddie would *have* to let her in—provided Whitney could find her way back to the cottage. The prospect of creeping among the blossoming citrus trees in the rain was not intriguing, but neither was staying put.

Her light fell on a steady stream of water flowing into her ragged leather satchel. "My music!" she groaned. Seeing her sixth book of Maxime Alphonse exercises curling under the rush of rain forced her into action.

With her horn tucked protectively under her arm, she collapsed the tent with everything still inside it, gathered up the open end, and slung it onto her back Santa Claus style. The weight was ungodly, and with her horn tucked under one arm and the flashlight held precariously in the hand of that same arm, she couldn't shift it around much. If she'd packed her horn in her hard case, she would have let it bounce around on her back with her other things, but, in its small, neat, soft case, it would have ended up hopelessly mangled.

"I shall prevail," she vowed aloud, and lumbered off.

Almost immediately she came to a fork in the road. Since she didn't even remember a fork in the road, she had no idea whether she should go left or right. Paddie had told her not to camp within a ten-minute walk of the cottage, and Whitney had obliged, heading out away from the cottage and the highway. She had assumed she would find her way back easily enough the following morning. But it was pitch dark and pouring rain now, and she could hardly remember her own name, never mind figure out how to find her way out of a citrus grove . . . and didn't alligators come out in the rain? Alligators and crocodiles were all the same to her. Snakes, too. Slimy reptiles.

Then, for some reason, she thought of Daniel Graham. Paddie wouldn't know a leaky tent from a spit rag, but Graham presumably would have realized the peril his trespasser would be in when the torrents started. Why hadn't he come to her rescue?

"Because, dope," she muttered to herself, "you don't look like the type that needs rescuing."

And, kiss aside, she undoubtedly hadn't endeared herself to the man with her lies. She would remember the kiss forever—it had been that kind of kiss, and he was that kind of man—but suspected he had forgotten it already. He'd simply taken advantage of an opportunity. He was *that* kind of man, too.

Blowing a drop of rain off the end of her nose, she reared back her shoulders, chose the fork to the left, and proceeded.

Within a hundred yards the grove ended and she was walking through an open clearing. A bona fide *lawn!* But it wasn't Paddie's lawn, and the house up ahead was much too large to be Paddie's cottage. A window on the second floor was lit, but otherwise the house was dark. Paddie didn't have a second floor. Off to the right, down a gentle slope, a small lake was spattered with raindrops.

Whitney stopped dead, ballet slippers squishing in the wet sand, sweat pants and hockey shirt heavy with the soaking rain, back and shoulders aching under the weight of her pack. The water beaded up and slid off her horn case. She could not envision herself marching up to Daniel Graham's front door and inviting herself in. It had to be his house. Her luck dictated it would be. Reason mandated that now she was on the edge of Daniel Graham's front lawn.

She could *not* ask him for help. He had seen her accursed tent! He had to know she was out there suffering, about to drown within spitting distance of his front porch, a woman he had kissed!

She whirled around, dropping the flashlight and nearly toppling over under the swinging weight of her pack. Her shoulders screamed. In the lake, bullfrogs croaked. Or was it an alligator?

Tears of exhaustion and frustration stung her eyes. She couldn't go back into the grove, either.

"Oh, blast it all," she muttered, retrieving her flashlight. "Daniel Graham beats an alligator—I think."

Straightening up as best she could, she stumbled across the lawn and, with heroic effort, trudged up his front steps. The door to the giant screened porch was unlocked. She went in. Her tent gave way, scattering her most precious possessions on the gray-painted floor. Clutching her horn to her, she raised her fist to pound on the inside door. She would demand human decency. She would—

Her flashlight touched upon a cozy-looking settee off to her right. A dark blue afghan was folded across the back. She paused, listening. Despite the racket she'd made, no one seemed to have stirred inside the house. She glanced at the mess she'd made and considered the mess she was in. Forget everything else—the burglary, the trespassing, the lies. Whatever else he might be, Daniel Graham *was* the chairman of the board of the Central Florida Symphony Orchestra, and she was taking over as its principal horn. That alone justified a little circumspection.

And, then, of course, there was the kiss. If she came tramping inside right now, what would happen? She was physically and mentally exhausted. She no longer dared to trust her instincts. Her willpower was nonexistent. If Daniel Graham offered her his bed, and him with it, she'd take them both.

The settee, she thought, would do just fine. She dug an unrevealing nightgown out of her suitcase and peeled off her wet, muddy clothes right there on the front porch. She left them in a heap and, with a few mumbled curses at Paddie, Daniel Graham, and herself, collapsed into a dead sleep.

Chapter Four

WHITNEY opened her eyes to the warmth of the sun angling in through the porch screen and the figure of Daniel Graham sitting in a wicker chair with the morning paper. He had on tan gabardine pants and a sparkling yellow cotton shirt. The sleeves weren't rolled up, but he hadn't yet fastened the buttons on the cuffs. His hair was dark and gleaming. Whitney peeked down at the floor. Even his damned shoes were polished! If she hadn't been so stiff and sleepy, she might have leaped off the settee and gone screaming into the grove. As it was, she drew the afghan up to her chin and yawned. She felt clammy and none too clean, and expected she looked it.

"Morning," he drawled.

At least he seemed to be in a good mood. And unarmed. There was a distinct twinkle in his eye that she found both compelling and unnerving. Even if he didn't, she remembered what had transpired, besides lies, between them last night. "Good morning," she said sedately. "How long have you been sitting there?"

"Long enough to read the sports section," he said with a smile that made her realize once again how spectacularly good-looking he was. Try as she would, she couldn't ignore his sensuality. It was there. Most assuredly, it was there. In heaps. He continued to smile and went on, "Nothing especially interesting unless you like golf. Do you?"

She shook her head. Wasn't he even curious about finding his thief and squatter asleep on his porch?

"I didn't think so. I haven't met a musician yet interested in sports."

"Hockey," she said through a yawn.

51

"I beg your pardon?"

"I'm a hockey fan. Ice hockey. I like the Buffalo Sabres."

"Ice hockey," he repeated. "I guess that explains your shirt."

Keeping the afghan tucked under her chin, she sat up slowly—and painfully. Her body ached. What she had needed last night was a warm bed and a hot shower. What she had gotten were a leaky tent and an inadequate settee . . . and a kiss that made her body ache in a different sort of way.

"Stiff?" Graham said, not concerned.

"A little," she lied. In the privacy of her own home she would have been groaning and cursing. "My tent leaked."

"Yes." He flipped a page in his newspaper. "I wondered how long it would take you to find your way back here."

"I had no idea I was camped so close to your house. I mean—" She stopped to think. She had to be careful not to give Paddie away. "I had no idea this was even your land. I—"

He eyed her humorously—sensually—over the top of the paper. "And I thought you were in love with me."

"Don't be funny, Mr. Graham," she said as haughtily as she could wrapped up in an afghan. "You know I'm not."

"Don't tell me you've changed your story again." He feigned surprise. "You'll have me spinning in so many directions I won't know which way is up."

"I'm sure you'd figure something out," she said wryly. "You're in a good mood, considering."

He laughed, and she wasn't sure she liked this irreverent individual she had woken up to any more than she had the wild-eyed man who had hauled her out of his closet. "Be glad I'm not having you drawn and quartered," he said languidly. "I tire of lies easily, Whitney. If you don't want to tell me what you're doing here, then don't. As I said, I have a feeling I know already. By the way, there's a bathroom through that door there and down the hall. Second door on the left."

How chivalrous of him to think of such things, Whitney thought dryly. But as she glanced around, she saw that her satchel, suitcase, canvas bag, and even her tent and flashlight were gone. So were her discarded sweat pants, hockey shirt, and pink ballet slippers. And her horn.

What if Paddie was right about him and he was some kind of murderous maniac and she was his prisoner and—

"My horn," she demanded, "what have you done with my horn?"

He folded the sports section, set it on the floor beside his chair, and picked up the real estate section. "First door on the left."

Paranoia doesn't suit me, Whitney told herself, and, seeing he was determined to be obtuse, she threw off the afghan, a little too hastily. Her gown had twisted around her thighs, revealing more of her long, winter-pale legs than she would have preferred in the company of a man she hardly knew and wasn't sure she wanted to know at all. Graham gave her legs, and her discomfiture, an amused glance. She huffed and stormed inside.

It was an elegant turn-of-the-century tan stucco house, and the first door on the left led to a lovely guest room with a cherry bed and a view of a flower garden. Pink azaleas bloomed in the window. Last night's rain had left them vibrant and glistening in the sun. Her suitcase, leather satchel, and canvas bag had all been brushed off, and her horn lay on the bed. The tent had vanished. So had her rain-soaked clothes. In the bathroom, towels and a fresh bar of apricot-scented soap were laid out.

Whitney immediately turned around, intending to tramp back out onto the porch, but Daniel Graham was there, leaning insolently against the bedroom door. "If this doesn't suit you," he said, "there are more rooms upstairs."

"Am I your houseguest or your prisoner?" she asked bluntly.

He laughed, moving into the room, standing close to her. She felt mussed, but his smile and the timbre of his laugh made her feel attractive. "Houseguest," he said. "I had the dungeon done over last winter. Nothing less would hold you, I'm sure."

"I thought you thought I was a thief."

She winced at her less than erudite statement, but forty-eight hours ago she had been in Schenectady whipping up a batch of scrambled eggs and wondering if she'd ever see Harry again. She'd missed him more than she had ever thought possible. A lot had happened during the past two days. She was tired.

"Not a thief," Daniel said mildly, "just a charming little liar." He ran a finger across the square line of her chin. "A very charming little liar."

"I was lots of things yesterday," she said, breathless, trying to pretend he wasn't standing so close, wasn't touching her, "but I didn't think charming was among them."

He laughed softly, his breath warm and strangely erotic on her mouth. "I find burglars in pink ballet slippers enormously charming—especially when they have mischievous blue eyes."

His finger brushed up along her cheek to the corner of her eye, massaging the tender skin there gently. Her lips were dry, but the rest of her felt warm and moist. Had she been a fool to come here?

"And I'm not little," she said valiantly. "I can't afford to be."

"You're hardly Harry Stagliatti, darlin'," Daniel drawled so deeply, so deliciously, that Whitney nearly lost her balance.

"True," she replied, quaking inside, but not with fear. No, definitely not with fear. "But I have to keep in shape. I do aerobic dance, lift weights, do yoga, run—"

"And practice that infernal instrument of yours."

Even his teasing was sexually tantalizing. His fingers wandered into her messy hair and brushed the smooth skin of the back of her neck. "Yes," she said, "lots. It requires a constant, controlled stream of air. I—I work hard to maintain and increase my lung capacity. It annoys me no end that all someone like Harry Stagliatti has to do is suck in air and blow."

"Is that all he does?"

"Well, no, I'm sure. I was just using him as an example."

"But you don't know him." It was a statement, slightly disbelieving.

"No, of course not. I— What are you doing?"

"Just what you want me to do," he replied innocently, smiling as he brought his mouth toward hers. "What we both want me to do."

She could have denied it then, if she had wanted to, but

instead she felt her lips part, felt her tongue licking them, and then his tongue, and his mouth, and his teeth, and she went into his arms. There was no horn between them now, and she could feel her breasts, unrestrained beneath the gown, pressing against his shirt. He drew her hard against him, his hands coursing down her spine, then cupping her buttocks and pulling her even more firmly against him. His long, lean, masculine body was outlined against hers. For the first time, she let her arms encircle his waist and feel the strength and hardness of his back. Her mouth opened wider, inviting a deepening of their kiss, answering the darting and probing of his tongue.

Then his hands slipped between them, touching the undersides of her breasts, and she moaned softly into his mouth until he held them freely in his palms, and then she moaned again.

"I shouldn't . . . ." she whispered hoarsely. "I can't . . ." *Harry, Paddie* . . .

Daniel pulled away, not sharply, but abruptly. "It's all right," he said at Whitney's look of surprise. "Darlin', believe me, it's all right. I only need to be asked once. You're not ready, I can see that."

"I don't even know you," she muttered. "I don't even know you, and yet—and yet this can happen."

He grinned roguishly. "Ain't life wonderful?"

"Yes, but . . ."

"Whitney, I sat out on that porch watching you for over an hour. I devised lots more than what just happened. Put it out of your mind, if you want." He started toward the door, but turned, his hand on the mahogany frame. His grin was still seductively roguish. "Me, I'll be mulling it over all morning. Make youself at home, darlin'."

The door shut softly behind him.

After showering and changing into a respectable pair of tan linen pants and a cream linen blouse, Whitney felt much more capable of reasoning with Daniel Graham, but his chair on the porch was empty. She called, but there was no answer. Then she saw the note scrawled above the *Orlando Sentinnel* masthead: "Had to go off into the cold, cruel world, but left humming. Be back later—be good. D. P.S. You can steal whatever you want from the fridge."

Whitney stuck her tongue out at the note, but when she headed back inside she realized she was humming, too. Handel's *Water Music.* She wondered if Daniel had hummed the same tune. Probably not.

The kitchen had been remodeled recently and was outfitted with gleaming modern appliances, but the big windows, the height of the ceilings, and the view of the blossoming orange grove gave the feel of old Florida. Whitney discovered a milk-white pitcher of fresh-squeezed orange juice in the refrigerator and made herself a pot of coffee and a couple of pieces of toast. Given the size and elegance of the house, she was surprised there wasn't an army of servants around. Daniel Graham, Whitney decided, was an unusual man. After her breakfast, she felt so good she decided she'd call Paddie at her office at the auditorium at Orlando Community College.

"Whitney!" Paddie exclaimed upon hearing her friend's voice. "You survived!"

"No thanks to you, Victoria. Why didn't you tell me I was camped out on Daniel Graham's land?"

Paddie hesitated, but only for a moment. "It would have caused you unnecessary fear and trepidation."

"You're damned right it would have!"

"You mean—"

"Yes, I mean! Our charming Mr. Graham caught me with my tent pitched under one of his damned orange trees!"

Whitney related her ordeal to an attentive Victoria Paderevsky, but Paddie's chagrin, if any, didn't last. "You're his houseguest?" she asked eagerly. "But this is wonderful! Now you can search his house, too."

"Victoria, you don't search your host's house. It just isn't done—"

"But you say he is not there."

"He isn't, but—"

"Then go quickly! You must act, Whitney. Maybe we can find out once and for all why he was in Mr. Stagliatti's rooms."

Mister? All day yesterday he had been just Harry. But Paddie hadn't been in her medium then. Now she was. Once they were hers, all musicians were *Mr., Miss,* or *Mrs.*

Paddie didn't believe in *Dr.* for anyone but herself, and she had decreed that *Ms.* sounded uneducated.

"Do you think Daniel would have invited me here if he had Harry tucked in the cellar?"

"Don't be ridiculous." Paddie sniffed. "Of course Graham wouldn't have left you alone if Mr. Stagliatti was a prisoner there! No, but perhaps you can find the things he took from Harry's room—or something. For heaven's sake, Whitney, take this opportunity to see if there *is* anything to find!"

"I'll know it when I see it?" Whitney suggested sourly.

"Exactly."

"Oh, Victoria! Daniel's innocent—"

"I was afraid he would have that effect on you." Paddie sighed, disgusted. "You must maintain your objectivity. Hurry. Call me when you've finished. No, wait. We will be in rehearsal then. We will finish at eleven-thirty. Call me then. By the way, can you make it to the four o'clock rehearsal? People think you are arriving today."

"They will also think I've just gotten off a plane. How could I play?"

"Yes, this is true," Paddie said reluctantly. "But you must come by the auditorium. I won't ask you to perform."

"Good of you."

"Yes," Paddie agreed. "Be cautious, Whitney."

Paddie had already hung up, and Whitney slammed the phone down. The woman was nuts! Daniel would figure out what Whitney was up to—indeed, it seemed he already had—and have *both* their heads. She sighed deeply. If only she hadn't seen that nasty drawing . . . and Paddie's face. Even brilliant, single-minded Victoria Paderevsky couldn't perform under that kind of pressure.

And Harry? His disappearance and the mind games someone was playing with Paddie weren't necessarily—or even obviously—connected. Harry was a fifty-seven-year-old adult male who could walk out on an orchestra if he damned well felt like it! It did not mean he'd been kidnapped.

And yet . . .

Whitney sighed. And yet could she take the chance that he *wasn't* in danger—and that Daniel was not involved?

Paddie had seen Daniel Graham in Harry's rooms! That had to mean *something*.

But what?

So Whitney did the only thing she could do: She searched Daniel Graham's house.

It was by no means a simple project. The house consisted of six bedrooms, a master suite, a library, an office, a study, a formal living room, a formal dining room, a pantry, a kitchen, two storage rooms, and four bathrooms. At first Whitney dawdled, enthralled by the straightforward elegance of the decor and the beauty of the view. Through every window she could see the endless rows of citrus trees, their gorgeous white blossoms glinting in the sunlight against their dark, waxy leaves. It was a magnificent sight. God's country, someone had called this part of Florida. On a morning such as this, Whitney could see why. In front of the house, the lake sparkled blue, with huge old cypress trees and pink dogwoods and white azaleas along its banks. Last night's rain, and all the fear and doubts that went with it, seemed far away.

But why had Daniel been parading through his property with a rifle slung over his shoulder? Corporate vice presidents and wealthy citrus growers didn't do such things. And his tale about poachers ranked with some of her lies. As far as the eye could see, the groves were in bloom. There was only that one section near Paddie's cottage where Whitney had actually seen any oranges. And whoever was harassing Paddie, it wasn't a poacher. How would a poacher know the faces of so many of the world's famous conductors? And how would a poacher know that that particular drawing would be so insulting, so degrading, to Victoria Paderevsky?

Whitney shoved her questions aside—and continued her search. In the large kitchen trash basket, she came upon her sweat pants and sweater. Gathering them up, she ran them through the wash. Now that she knew her way around the big house, she felt quite at home.

Dennis Brain was belting out the third movement of Mozart's Horn Concerto No. 4 in E-flat and Whitney was humming along, picking through the trash for any clues, thinking she should be practicing her horn, when the back door opened and Daniel and an older man and woman walked in. The woman was well into middle age, almost as tall as he was, with the same straight, somewhat arrogant-looking nose. She wore a teal-blue suit and good shoes, and she was the kind of woman who made Whitney wonder if she'd ever grow up. The other man was short and heavy-set, dressed in a blue seersucker suit.

Whitney tucked a wispy curl behind her ear, gathered up her collection of trash, dumped it into the bright yellow basket, and smiled at her host, who pointedly did not smile back. "Hello," she said cheerfully, "I was just looking for my earring. I thought I dropped one into the trash."

"Don't let us disturb you." Daniel's voice was almost genial; his eyes were anything but. Her stomach fluttered annoyingly; the man had an undeniable physical effect on her. He turned to the two beside him. "Mother, Tom, why don't you go into the dining room and wait there? I'll be along in a minute."

"Is there anything I can do?" his mother asked with a furtive glance down at Whitney. "I don't believe I know your friend."

Whitney crawled to her feet. "I'm—"

"She's Sara Jones, Mother," Daniel said quickly, "my new maid. Sara, this is Rebecca Graham, my mother, and Thomas Walker, a friend of the family's."

"Delighted to meet you, Miss Jones," Thomas said.

"Likewise," Rebecca said politely. "I've been telling Daniel for months he should get someone in full time to help with this place. If you'll excuse us . . ."

"Well," Daniel said when they'd gone, "did you find anything?"

"My earring, you mean? Nope."

"You have two darling little pearls in your ears, sweet-heart."

She rinsed her hands off in the sink. "You shouldn't call your maid *sweetheart.*"

"Damn it, Whitney," he said sharply.

"Sara," she corrected, taking a hand towel and turning to him. "Remember?"

"I could wring your neck!"

His voice was low and menacing, but for some inexplicable reason Whitney wasn't the least nonplussed. He glared at her, and all she could think of was how spectacular he looked all dressed up in his tan gabardine suit. "And I thought the *real* Daniel Graham was not interested in kissing my neck," she said lightly.

"Don't push your luck, Whitney," he grunted. "You searched my house, didn't you?"

She took great care in wiping her hands. "What gave you that idea?"

"That's my record playing, isn't it?"

"And your trash I picked through—not enough evidence for your conclusion, Mr. Graham. And I'll have you know you threw away a perfectly good set of clothes. I rescued them."

"You're trying my patience."

"So fire me."

He sighed heavily and rubbed his forehead as if he had a migraine. She noticed the fine yellow cotton of his shirt and the understated madras tie he had added. The tanned skin above his collar drew her eye, and she noted every last detail of his lean, muscular physique. This has to stop, she thought, wondering if another piece of toast and marmalade would help the funny feeling in the pit of her stomach.

"I'd like to stick your butt on a plane back to Schenectady," he grumbled, "but things are in enough of a mess as it is."

Whitney draped the towel over the edge of the sink. "I appreciate your concern," she said dryly, "but I assure you I can handle my own butt."

For an instant she saw the glint of humor in his eyes. "Can you now?"

She couldn't resist an answering glint of humor in her own eyes. The man didn't need to resort to nasty tricks to drive a woman crazy! "Why did you lie about me?" she asked, sounding much more placid than her insides suggested she was. "They'll find out sooner or later I'm not your maid, you know."

"Same reason you've been lying to me, Whitney," he replied, pushing the tails of his jacket back in yet another pose Whitney found impossibly sensual. She could see the expensive leather belt and the enticing line of his narrow hips. "Expediency. And, by the way, don't think I've forgotten about your lies. You still owe me one hell of an explanation, sweetheart."

"I've been trying to think up a new one all morning," she said airily.

Daniel was not amused. "I want the truth this time, Whitney. And you *are* going to tell me."

"Or?"

"Pray it doesn't come to that."

"You're not as intimidating without your assorted weapons."

"Shall I get them out?" But he couldn't hold back a smile.

"There's no need," she said with a sniff. "I know where they are."

"Damn it, you did search my house!"

"Every nook and cranny. I like your bathroom, by the way. But I thought everyone in Florida was water-conscious. You could bathe an entire harem in that tub. Who knows, maybe you have."

Daniel sucked in a deep, sharp breath. "I can't wait to see you go up against Dr. Paderevsky," he muttered. "After you, Harry will seem downright tame. Whitney, you know I won't hurt you—I only want you to talk to me."

"The feeling's mutual, Daniel."

"All right, then we'll talk, but first I have another mess to sort out. My mother and Thomas both sit on the orchestra's board of directors. Why I ever agreed to become chairman is totally beyond me, but I suppose it'll be good for our community image—unless Dr. Paderevsky doesn't straighten out." He broke off with a clipped hiss. "Look, Whitney, in about ten minutes several people from the orchestra are going to be here. As far as I know, they still think you're not arriving until this afternoon. My life would be much simpler if they continue under that impression."

"Frankly, so would mine."

"I had a feeling you'd agree," he said coolly.

Whitney sighed. "One minute the man's cursing me to the rafters and the next he wants a favor—"

"Would you prefer I tied you up and stuffed you in the pantry? This is not a game, Whitney."

"*You're* telling me? Who, may I ask, has been physically assaulted and interrogated at gunpoint?"

"I did not assault you."

"You—"

"Whitney, I don't have time. Will you please make yourself scarce?"

She folded her arms stubbornly across her chest. "What's the meeting about? Has Dr. Paderevsky—"

"None of your damned business. Now go on and get, will you?"

She just managed to dodge a motivating slap on the rump. Or, as he would say, butt. "Okay, okay," she said, "but who's going to make coffee?"

He shook his head, exasperated. "I can manage."

Whitney grinned on her way out the kitchen door. "With a full-time maid at your beck and call? I'd like to hear you explain that one to your mother."

She was quite sure only the sound of a car engine in the driveway prevented him from coming after her.

Chapter Five

From a crack in her bedroom door, Whitney watched the people parade into the dining room for Daniel's mysterious meeting. She felt a great sense of foreboding as she began to recognize faces. She instantly spotted Yoshifumi Kamii, the brilliant concertmaster of the CFSO, and Angelina Carter, the principal flutist, both of whom Whitney had known during her days in New York City. There were also associate conductor and principal violist Bradley Fredericks, whom she thought she recognized, and a tall, lanky black man she suspected might be principal cellist Lucas Washington. A youngish tawny-haired man followed them into the hall, greeted everyone in a friendly drawl, and, beaming, held the swinging dining room door open for Angelina. Whitney assumed him to be the likable Matthew Walker, general manager of the CFSO. Now *he*, she thought, was handsome and chivalrous.

Normally Whitney didn't spy on other people's conversations, but this time she knew she had to. The one person who should have been at any meeting between members of the orchestra and the board of directors wasn't there: Victoria Paderevsky. And as irritating as the woman could be, Whitney was very definitely on her side. So, like any good maid, Whitney tiptoed out to the closed double dining room doors and listened at the keyhole.

"You must understand," Yoshifumi was saying in his distinctive Tokyo accent, "that we are acting out of concern for Dr. Paderevsky. We are not trying to undermine her authority."

It was almost twelve-thirty, Whitney thought. They

must have come directly from rehearsal—at Paddie's request? It didn't sound like it.

"But you're meeting here without her knowledge," Daniel Graham pointed out.

"Only because we don't know what else to do," Angelina said, her voice recognizable by virtue of her being the only woman present except for Rebecca Graham, who had a Southern accent.

"Have you tried talking to Dr. Paderevsky?" Rebecca asked.

There was a stunned silence. At least Whitney assumed it was stunned. *No one* talked to Paddie.

"We thought we would meet with you people first," Yoshifumi said.

"I recommended it." The nasal, cultured accent confirmed that Bradley Fredericks was in fact present. He was Boston born and bred and sounded it. "I had hoped we could keep this informal and—"

"Quiet?" Daniel suggested.

"Well, yes."

"All right," he said with a touch of impatience. Whitney was beginning to recognize all the nuances of his deep drawl. "Talk to me."

And they did. Victoria Paderevsky was a difficult personality, but a brilliant conductor. This, the musicians said, was common knowledge. When they agreed to come to Orlando to found the Central Florida Symphony Orchestra under her direction, they knew what to expect: long hours, fits of temper, unrealistically high expectations, an ulcer or two, but, ultimately, a world-class orchestra. In short, they both despised and respected Paddie.

During the past week, however, Paddie's behavior had begun to change. "I don't know how to explain it," Yoshifumi said, "but she's just not . . . invincible, I guess."

"She looks tired," Angelina said.

"My God," Daniel interrupted, "the woman's been working night and day for months! What do you expect?"

"You have to understand," Bradley went on, "that Dr. Paderevsky is positively religious about getting eight hours of sleep each night. She doesn't have a social life and would never risk the quality of her work by attending a rehearsal in a state of exhaustion. This week, however, she's complained about staying up too late and awaking at dawn."

"The lady's not your basic insomniac type," someone drawled—Lucas Washington, Whitney assumed; he was from Atlanta and getting him was another of Paddie's impossible coups.

She could hear Daniel's irritated sigh through the door, but there was more. During break on Monday, Paddie had spit coffee all over Yoshifumi, but denied that anything was wrong with her or the coffee. Afterward she was so distracted she came out with the wrong score. On Tuesday she was called away in the middle of rehearsal for an important phone call—what in Paddie's life could be more important than a rehearsal?—and returned almost immediately, looking haggard and drawn. The janitor had been outside her office and said Paddie had listened all of three seconds before she told the caller to leave her alone and hung up.

"This has all been happening since Harry Stagliatti decided to miss a few rehearsals, hasn't it?" Whitney was sure she recognized Thomas Walker's cultured drawl. "Well, perhaps she's just worried others will follow his lead and is trying to show you, in her own way, that she is human. I've been expecting something like this myself. As Daniel says, she's been going flat out. She's never had total responsibility for a major orchestra before. She's young, inexperienced, and—"

"We know your prejudices, Father," a male voice—Matthew Walker's—said with strained pleasantry.

"Yes, Matthew," Thomas said, "and we all know you're supposed to be general manager of this orchestra. Doesn't that woman listen to you?"

"Frankly," Rebecca Graham interrupted, picking up the threads of the conversation, "I wouldn't think Mr. Stagliatti's departure would have this kind of effect on Dr. Paderevsky. He *said* he'd be back, didn't he?"

"Yes," Yoshifumi said, "but he left abruptly, and apparently without reason. Dr. Paderevsky has a right to be angry, but we're concerned that more than anger is involved."

"They weren't close, were they?" Rebecca asked, surprised.

The musicians all answered no. Whitney tried not to laugh. If only Harry were here!

"Matthew," Daniel said, "what do you think?"

"Losing Harry one week before opening night has been a terrible blow," he said, pausing to clear his throat, "especially with the premiere program featuring the horn section."

"Oh, come on, son," Thomas Walker put in. "Dr. Paderevsky must know horn players are a dime a dozen."

Whitney decided she didn't like Thomas Walker. Resisting an urge to kick down the doors and choke him, she gritted her teeth and rubbed the ache in her back. What did that idiot know about horn players?

"Truly fine hornists are not a dime a dozen," Yoshifumi said. "However, I believe that Dr. Paderevsky's problem goes deeper than a simple reaction to the walkout of one of her musicians. I could be wrong, of course, but my instincts tell me otherwise."

Smart man, Yoshifumi, Whitney thought.

"What you're saying," Daniel said, "is that you think Dr. Paderevsky is cracking."

"We're just alerting you to a potential problem," Angelina replied, businesslike. "There is one other incident you should be aware of. I'm not sure it means anything myself, but . . . well, at this morning's practice, Dr. Paderevsky told us that Whitney McCallie, Harry's replacement— We think she's replacing Harry a little prematurely, but never mind that. Anyway, Whitney's supposed to be arriving this afternoon, and she—Dr. Paderevsky, that is—was actually nice. I don't know how to explain this. Lucas, you were there."

"The lady described Whitney as her 'one true friend,' which just isn't how the doctor talks, you know?"

It certainly wasn't, Whitney thought. Paddie *was* cracking up! Whoever was trying to drive her crazy had already succeeded.

"Dr. Paderevsky and Miss McCallie know one another?" Daniel asked.

"Certainly," Bradley Fredericks said.

"That's right," Yoshifumi added. "The only senior performance recital Dr. Paderevsky ever attended was Whitney's. They were great friends."

Passing acquaintances, Yoshifumi, Whitney thought, straightening up and preparing to make her escape. But to where? She could *not* let Daniel pick her brains before she'd talked to Paddie. They would have to confide in him, but that wasn't a decision Whitney could, in good conscience, make alone.

"I see," Daniel said tightly. "Do any of you know Miss McCallie?"

"Oh, sure," Yoshifumi said, adding another nail to her coffin. "She's a great horn player—not a Harry Stagliatti, you understand, or Paddie would have gotten her in the first place. But a few more years with Harry and she'll be right up there with him. Even he says so, and he doesn't have much good to say about any of his students. It's her tone."

"Any of his students?" Daniel asked sharply. "What do you mean?"

"You didn't know? I figured Paddie would have told you. Whitney is Harry's top student. They've been together—I don't know, ten years?"

"I see," Daniel said again, even more tightly.

"Daniel," Matthew Walker said, "after consulting with a few representatives of the orchestra about Dr. Paderevsky's odd behavior, I decided perhaps I should talk to Whitney before she arrived. I called the airline and learned she's already here in Florida. She arrived yesterday. It seems to me there's something going on around here that I haven't been told about. Would you happen to know anything about it?"

Whitney could hear Daniel's heavy, irritated sigh through the solid door. "I don't know any reason beyond overwork and Harry's apparent walkout for any change in Dr. Paderevsky's behavior. It seems to me we're all on edge. Give her the weekend to relax and see what happens. As for Miss McCallie, she did arrive unexpectedly yesterday"—to say the least, Whitney thought—"and is staying here as my houseguest. I thought since she was coming on such short notice she might need a place to stay. Other than that, I don't know what to tell you. I had no idea she and Dr. Paderevsky were friends."

Whitney winced at the condemnation in his tone. Thanks to her comrades, she had more explaining to do

than ever. She didn't blame Daniel for being angry. He
was sitting in there putting all the little pieces together
and realizing just how much lying Whitney had done. But
what choice had she had?

She uncrooked her back and stretched painfully. And
what choice did she have now? This was no time for Whitney to abandon Paddie. Whitney could function without
the respect and support of the CFSO; Paddie couldn't, no
matter what she thought.

Someone suggested Daniel fetch Whitney in to talk to
them. She didn't wait to hear his answer, but stole upstairs, knowing what she had to do. Before they dug their
hole any deeper—and definitely before Whitney ended up
alone and at the mercy of Daniel Graham—Paddie and
Whitney had to consult. Whitney would urge Paddie to tell
Daniel everything. Then they would go on from there.

But first Whitney had to get to Paddie.

"Before Daniel gets to me," she muttered as she slipped
into his bedroom.

During her search that morning, she had noted the set of
keys on his dresser. She seized them now and ran quietly
back downstairs, sneaking out through the front door onto
the porch. When she finally did explain, she hoped Daniel
would understand.

It was a sunny, warm day, and she would have liked
nothing better than to sit out on a lounge chair and practice her horn and recuperate from yesterday. But, Whitney
thought, duty called.

She cut around back. There were several cars parked on
the blacktop, but only one, a dark green Porsche, looked
like Daniel Graham. The key fit, and, after stalling out
twice and wondering constantly if she was doing the right
thing, off she roared.

Now, she thought glumly, Daniel had her for breaking
and entering, trespassing, and car stealing. Only, of
course, she wasn't stealing, she was borrowing. She hoped
their kisses had meant something after all and he was
willing to make such distinctions . . . *when* she explained.

Orlando Community College was a gleaming, modern
campus on the southeast side of the burgeoning city. Signs
of new, rapid, and not always sensible growth were every-

where: housing developments, construction, shopping centers, apartment complexes, neon signs, real estate agents. Whitney found herself mysteriously longing for the signs of the old, slowed down, and not always sensible growth of upstate New York. But, she reminded herself as she parked the Porsche in the shade of an oak, there was seventeen inches of snow on the ground in Schenectady. And no Disney World.

The Porsche was a sensitive car. Her four-wheel-drive Subaru back in Schenectady was not. And that, she decided, explained why she had stalled out three times on her way over from Daniel's place, which she had finally figured out was west of Orlando. She got lost twice, but having weary attendants at service stations explain just exactly where she was helped her find the college. Promising herself she would study the maps each of the attendants had thrust at her, Whitney finally parked the car and headed up a sidewalk flanked with azaleas and dogwoods.

The auditorium—Graham Auditorium, naturally—was connected to the main administration building. Whitney got herself yet another map from an information booth and found her way through the maze of halls. She entered the auditorium on Level B behind the last row of seats. Except for a single light which lit the unoccupied stage below, the auditorium was dark. The door behind her banged shut automatically. Whitney jumped, startled, and chastised herself for her nervousness. She'd been in dark concert halls before.

It was bigger than she had expected, deep, and, although there was no balcony, traditionally designed. The seats were cushioned and covered with a red fabric, and there were three carpeted aisles. The stage seemed to have ample room for a full-scale symphonic orchestra. Paddie's office would be on Level A, probably somewhere behind the stage. Whitney sucked in a breath and moved silently down the steep far-right aisle.

She felt the movement behind her before she heard it. There was no time to react. Something compact and hard pressed into the small of her back. A muffled voice—eerie and without accent, neither male nor female—told her not to turn around.

"Why are you here?" the neutered voice demanded.

"Me?"

"Yes, you! Why?"

"I'm just the new horn player," she replied carefully. That this wasn't Daniel was beyond doubt. He of the kick-ass-and-take-names school of diplomacy would not have been able to restrain himself.

"I know who you are." The voice was more emphatic, angry, but not louder. The hard object pressed more firmly into Whitney's back. A gun? The point of a knife? "And I know what you're doing. It has to stop. Do you hear me? You'll only get hurt."

Thank you, Paddie, Whitney thought, for telling your entire orchestra—a member of which could be a maniac—that I'm your one true friend. "Okay," she said. "Sure. I'll—"

Then, down below, a side door opened, light angling into the darkened abyss of the concert hall, and Daniel Graham's voice bellowed, "McCallie? Damn it, woman, enough's enough!"

She moaned to herself and thought, *I'm dead . . .*

The pressure on her back withdrew and she started to whirl around to face her attacker, but, without any warning, she was shoved forward, headlong down the aisle. Her arms and legs flailed wildly as she tried to keep her balance, but she had been pushed hard. She fell, rolling like a log, just as the overhead lights came on.

She came to a dead stop in a crumpled-up heap at Daniel's feet.

"What in the name of hell do you think you're doing?" he yelled, catching her by the elbows and snapping her to her feet. "Damn it, I knew you'd come here—"

"Did you see him—her—it—" She flew around as best she could in Daniel's iron embrace. "Don't just stand here! Let's go after him!"

His fingers crushed into her upper arms, and she looked back at his angry, slanted eyes. "It won't work," he said.

"Daniel, damn it! Someone had a gun to my back and just knocked me down and—and—" She thought of Paddie and clamped her mouth shut. Maybe Paddie was right and Daniel *was* the one out to ruin her. Maybe he did have Harry locked up somewhere. Maybe whoever had just attacked Whitney was working with Daniel Graham. Since when had she been any judge of character? She was far too easygoing to trust her instincts about people. "Nothing. Never mind. I just tripped."

Daniel's grip softened, but he didn't release her. Instead he slowly, almost absently, massaged her upper arms. It was very distracting. Whitney forgot her doubts about him. They made less sense, were less real, than what her mind and heart were telling her now—what Daniel was telling her, without words. She began to feel warm and safe and imagined what it would be like just to lay her head on his chest and have his arms go around her back.

"Whitney," he said quietly, "you're lying again."

"I'm not."

"You get a distant look in those big blue eyes of yours when you're telling a tale." He brushed her cheek and gently touched his thumb to her lower lip. "No one pushed you and you didn't trip. You came here to see your *friend* Dr. Paderevsky, didn't you? We all heard you race off in my car, Whitney. Here I'm trying to calm people down and you're stirring up trouble."

She shrugged, a noble but failed attempt to seem nonchalant. She'd just been attacked—again—and now Daniel Graham was stroking her arms and mouth and cheek and looking at her with such softness and understanding that she almost *did* lay her head on his chest. What would he do if she did? she wondered. What would she do?

"How did you get here?" she asked.

"Yoshifumi gave me a ride." He tucked a lock of her hair behind her ear and grinned. "I'm afraid he no longer thinks I'm the perfect Southern gentleman. I cursed you rather soundly. Whitney, Whitney, who besides me would want to knock you down?"

"Exactly what I was wondering," she said.

He laughed softly. "Whitney, Whitney." His mouth lowered and barely touched her lips. Her pulse quickened, but it had nothing to do with fear now. He had a peculiar way of putting the attack and her lingering terror out of her mind. "You do strange things to me, Whitney McCallie," he said, his breath warm on her mouth. He stood back, dropping his hands to his sides, and smiled. "Relax . . .

there's no one there," he said with a nod toward the back of the auditorium.

His persistent doubt was thinly disguised. It rankled, especially after their kiss. And *most* especially because she had enjoyed the feel and promise of that brief contact. "Of course there isn't now that you've come barreling in here!" she said tartly.

"Then you should thank me for saving your life."

"You did not save my life—at least I don't think you did. I never thought my life was threatened and—" She sighed, aggravated. "In any case, you didn't mean to do anything heroic."

"You're right," he admitted, unchastened. "I meant to have your head for stealing my car, but you, as usual, devised a bizarre method to distract me."

She wrinkled up her face. "Borrow," she said. "I don't steal—and I didn't come tumbling down the aisle just to play on your sympathies. You yourself said I'm not a convincing femme fatale. Someone *did* accost me."

"Why would someone accost you?" he asked languidly, but not quite absently.

"Because—" She saw the trap just in time; Daniel was looking remarkably cool and alert. "How would I know? I'm the new girl in town, remember?"

"Whitney . . ." He raked his fingers through his hair, making it look even more wild and tousled. "We need to talk," he added simply.

"You mean *I* need to talk and you'll listen."

"Are you always this belligerent?"

"Only when a man kisses me and accuses me of lying all within two minutes."

"And theft, don't forget," he said with a small smile.

"I haven't forgotten."

His face broke into a grin, and she wondered how a man could be so exasperating and appealing at the same time. "The kiss was the best part, don't you think?" He chucked her under the chin in a gesture that was at once playful and hopelessly sensual. "You stick in a man's mind, you know."

Whitney was beginning to feel warm all over again, which, under the circumstances, was totally inappropriate. Being around Daniel Graham was emotionally exhausting—and physically trying. She dipped her hand into her pants pocket, fished out his keys, and handed them over. "I would have left a note, but all that stuff about horn players being a dime a dozen goaded me into insane action." When he scowled at her, she grinned unabashedly. "Am I getting a distant look in my big blue eyes?"

"Very," he said dryly. "Do you plan to report your 'attack'?"

"I just did," she said lightly. "You're the chairman of the board. If you think the police ought to be called in, call them. I wouldn't want the orchestra to get any undue negative publicity." Her sarcasm was not subtle. She cocked her chin up at Daniel. "Would you?"

"One difficult woman in this orchestra is enough," he muttered.

"Humph," Whitney said, sounding like Paddie herself.

As if in spite of himself, Daniel laughed—a short, deep, sensual laugh that licked the small of Whitney's back, erasing all memory of the pressure of that hard, threatening object. He recovered all too quickly, straightening up and looking very corporate in his immaculate suit. He was an intriguing combination of personalities, she thought: virile and utterly masculine, sensitive and thoughtful, teasing and fun. But why was she thinking of such things now?

"I think I'll forego calling the police for now," he said formally. "I would think whoever attacked you is long gone and you can't provide a description. Or can you?"

Her heart skipped. "Do you or don't you believe me?"

He smiled. "I'm keeping my options open."

Or did he know something she didn't know? Was he testing her? Maybe a conniving, skillful kidnapper was another facet of his personality. *Oh, don't be ridiculous!* But weren't psychopaths impossible to tell from normal people? She pushed the thought aside. She liked Daniel. *And* she had searched his home and office and found nothing damning.

"Whitney?"

"Hmm? Oh. Sorry. I was in a fog. No, I can't provide a description. I never saw anyone. You don't think— Could it have been a practical joke? Sort of an initiation or something?"

Daniel looked thoughtful, his mouth drawn straight, then twisting slowly to one side. "It's possible," he admitted. "Six months ago I would have said definitely not, but six months ago I didn't know a great deal about musicians and their sense of humor. What do you think?"

"I don't know."

"Care to tell me what was said?"

"Oh, just what you'd expect." She averted her eyes so he couldn't see if they had a distant look in them or not. "The voice was pretty muffled, so I couldn't hear very well—something about my being in town early."

"Apparently I'm not the only one who finds that suspicious."

"Apparently."

"Whitney, you have a few things to explain to me—and don't try to look vapid because you're not. You're Harry Stagliatti's student and Victoria Paderevsky's friend, and, damn it, I want to know what you were doing in my office yesterday!" He drew in a breath. "You're going to talk to me, darlin' dear."

He took her arm, but she hesitated. "People have such strange ideas about me. Wait, I should check in with Paddie . . ."

" 'Paddie' doesn't expect you until this afternoon, remember?" He sounded skeptical—as if he didn't believe for a second that Paddie didn't already know her new principal horn was in town, which, under the circumstances, Whitney thought perfectly reasonable.

She decided it was prudent to stick with her lie. She could blame it all on Paddie later. "Yes, but if she hears I've arrived and didn't come see her at once and—"

She was interrupted by the clattering of music stands on the stage above them, and then Paddie's stout figure stamped down the stairs. "Whitney!" she cried out. "You are here! Welcome."

Daniel glanced sideways down at Whitney. "Recognized you right off the bat, didn't she?" he said in a low, sarcastic voice. "Rather odd, I would think, for someone you don't know personally."

Whitney ignored him. "Vic— Dr. Paderevsky, how are you? It's so good to see you."

She thought her polite words and Daniel Graham's

menacing, skeptical look would tip Paddie off, but subtleties —unless musical—rarely worked with the brilliant conductor. However, this time Paddie picked it up. "You are early, yes? Good! Now you can come to the four o'clock rehearsal."

"Dr. Paderevsky . . ."

"Yes, you must come. We all miss Mr. Stagliatti, of course, the ingrate, but this program could have been tailored for you, Whitney. *Till,* Beethoven's Seventh, *Firebird*—you will do beautifully. Ah, Whitney, wait until you hear my orchestra."

Whitney could feel Daniel stiffening at her side, but couldn't decide which of Paddie's comments he found most offensive. "I look forward to it," she replied.

"I see you've met Mr. Graham," Paddie said. "He's our chairman of the board—very good to us, yes. How are you, Mr. Graham?"

"Fine," he said, "just fine."

"Dr. Paderevsky," Whitney said, "I was wondering if we could get together for a few minutes—"

"Three-thirty," Paddie interrupted. "I will be in my office. Be prompt."

"Dr. Paderevsky, Ms. McCallie," Daniel said, businesslike, "I want to see you both after rehearsal—seven o'clock at the latest. Meet me back at the house." He looked from one woman to the other. "I suggest you be there."

Paddie fastened her beady eyes on him. "I do not take that kind of order from you, Mr. Graham."

"You damned well better tonight."

Even if Paddie hadn't seen him skulking around Harry's room, Whitney understood why Paddie had picked Daniel for her number-one suspect. The man had no personal finesse. Of course, neither did Paddie. Whitney debated trying to make peace between them, but by the time she decided it wasn't worth the effort Paddie had stomped off and Daniel had banged through the door he'd come in. She was left alone in the big auditorium. Just as she started to fume, she remembered the episode on Level B and got the creeps.

She raced out into the lobby, but Daniel was gone. By the time she reached the parking lot, so was his Porsche.

She was without transportation. And her horn was back at
his house. A cab was going to cost her a fortune!

"To hell with it," she muttered.

It was time Paddie accepted some responsibility for
Whitney's health and welfare. The least she could do was
to drive Whitney out to pick up her horn.

She went back to the auditorium—this time walking
around the outside of the main building and entering the
lobby, then cutting down a hall and going behind stage.
Paddie's office was easy to find because it was the only one
with a name on it. Just V. PADEREVSKY. The door was standing open, but Paddie wasn't in. Whitney found a felt-tip
pen and a sheet of music paper on the cluttered desk and
started to write a note: "Found nothing, but much to tell
you when you decide to listen. Won't be . . ."

There was a sound, a movement, and then a sudden,
searing pain at the back of her neck.

And then nothing.

Chapter Six

THROUGH the haze of pain, Whitney could hear voices—a man and a woman arguing. Her name was mentioned; something about burglars. The man's voice was closer. She swallowed. Her throat was dry. Her head ached. As consciousness returned, she fought the pain and the fear and the wave of dizziness. She was lying on something soft and clammy—a vinyl couch? Then she remembered. There was a vinyl couch, cluttered with music and folders, in Paddie's office.

Paddie . . . Daniel . . .

"How was I to know she wasn't a burglar?" Paddie was saying.

"For God's sake," Daniel Graham barked, "you just saw her ten minutes ago!"

Paddie sniffed, indignant. "I did not recognize her."

"Terrific."

Whitney could feel two strong hands on her waist. A man's hands. Daniel's. She kept her eyes closed, half because she was sure opening them would only worsen the throbbing ache in her head, half because she was perfectly lucid and wanted to hear what Paddie and Daniel had to say. Paddie was trying to convince Daniel she had hit Whitney, but she was using her fake Lithuanian accent, which meant she was probably lying. But why? And where had Daniel come from?

"Whitney," he said softly, "are you all right?"

Paddie scoffed. "I did not hit her that hard."

Whitney opened one eye and winced in agony. "Ouch," she said, and tried to smile.

Daniel smiled back, tenderly. He was down on one knee

77

next to the couch. Things were scattered over the floor. Paddie stood behind him, scowling. He touched Whitney's chin gently with one finger. "You've got a nasty bump," he said. "Dr. Paderevsky, it seems, mistook you for a burglar."

"A lot of that's been going around lately," Whitney said, trying to sit up—but too soon. She felt the blood drain out of her head. "I think I'm going to throw up . . ."

Paddie groaned in disgust, but Daniel slipped an arm over her shoulders, steadying her. She sank her head against his chest and felt the wave of nausea dissipate. In its place came a peculiar, unexpected sense of belonging. Daniel smelled faintly of cologne and cotton fabric. His chest was a nice, solid place to rest.

"Shall I call a doctor?" he asked.

"No!" Paddie shrieked.

Beneath her cheek, Whitney could feel Daniel's chest expand as he took in a deep breath, the stiffening that began there and moved through the rest of his long body. Yet he asked in a controlled drawl, "Why not?"

"The publicity . . ."

"I'm all right," Whitney interrupted, lifting her head off Daniel's chest. "I wasn't out for very long, I don't think."

"Not even a minute," Paddie declared.

Daniel ignored Paddie and concentrated on Whitney. "You could have a concussion."

"Impossible," Paddie pronounced.

Whitney grimaced, wishing Paddie would just keep her mouth shut for five minutes. She had to think. "I agree with Victoria," she mumbled.

"My," Daniel said dryly, "what a surprise."

"About a concussion—I'm sure I don't have one. I wasn't hit that hard."

But she was quite sure Paddie hadn't hit her. In spite of her well-developed sense of the dramatic, she wasn't the type to knock someone on the head—especially the wrong someone. But why was she taking the blame? Just so Daniel wouldn't start asking questions about who *had* hit Whitney and go to the police? Whitney scowled. Paddie's orchestra be damned, she thought. She wanted to know who had hit her and why!

Daniel helped her sit up against the cool vinyl back of

the couch. She folded her hands across her thighs in a show of stoicism. What she wanted to do was roll around and moan in agony. She *hurt!* After seeing she would survive, Daniel circled round Paddie's desk. The office was small, windowless, and messy. A CFSO poster was taped to the wall behind the desk. Daniel looked aggravated enough to strangle his world-famous conductor, but all he did was give her a black look and pick up the phone. It was becoming clear to Whitney, if not to Paddie, that he did in fact want Victoria Paderevsky on the podium opening night—although he had to be having his doubts. In any case, any lingering suspicions Whitney might have had faded and died: Daniel Graham wasn't out to drive Paddie nuts.

Paddie wrinkled up her face at him and squatted down beside Whitney. "I am sorry I hit you," she said. "It was an accident."

"It's all right." Whitney's words of reassurance were for Daniel's benefit. For now, she thought it prudent to present a unified front. From her look, Paddie had already guessed Whitney knew she was lying. "But what will your orchestra say?"

"What they are already saying," Paddie replied with a philosophical shrug of her heavy shoulders. "That the ugly conductor is crazy."

"You're not crazy, Victoria."

"*I* know." She grinned, her face lighting up. "But I am ugly, yes?"

"Oh, Victoria."

"Ha, that is what I like about you, Whitney: no platitudes. I—" She whirled around, instantly alert and antagonistic, and leaped to her feet. She shook her fists at Daniel. *"What did you say?"*

Daniel ignored her and continued speaking into the telephone. "If anyone has any questions, you're to repeat the following statement: 'In order to give orchestra members ample opportunity to rest before the premiere of the CFSO, afternoon rehearsals are being rescheduled. Beginning today, there will be no four o'clock rehearsals. Beginning Monday, there will be one afternoon rehearsal, starting at two o'clock. We apologize for the short notice but feel certain this will meet with your approval. Have a good weekend.' In fact, Louise, why don't you do that up in a memo? Thanks."

Paddie was turning purple. Sure she was going to have a heart attack, Whitney crawled to her feet and promptly collapsed, her knees buckling under her.

"You can't do this," Paddie sputtered, oblivious to Whitney's problem.

"I just did," Daniel replied calmly. He came around from behind the desk and easily lifted Whitney into his arms. "You're going to the doctor, sweetheart," he informed her, taking charge.

Paddie threw something. Whitney heard it hit the wall and crash to the floor. *"Daniel Graham, I am the music director of this orchestra!"*

"And I'm the chairman of the board," he replied with a calm that Whitney knew would only further inflame Paddie. "And, in spite of what you two seem to think, I'm also on your side. Now shut up, Paddie, and help me get Whitney to a doctor. Or do you want to have to scour the countryside for another principal horn?"

Suddenly Paddie looked crushed. "Is she hurt that badly?"

"If she has a concussion, I doubt she'll be able to play."

Now he was hitting Paddie where she'd notice. "I don't have a concussion," Whitney managed lamely.

Daniel told her to shut up, too, and scooped her all the way up in his arms. She felt as light and carefree as a baked meringue—a pleasant, if elusive, feeling. Paddie argued that Whitney could walk and that if anyone saw him carrying her around, there would be talk. Daniel snapped back that there already *was* talk; this would just make the talk juicier. Paddie growled and heaved a pen at the wall. Daniel turned nimbly, Whitney in his arms, and walked toward the door.

Then, just as they were leaving, he turned and said offhandedly, "Oh, by the way, Paddie, maybe you ought to bring along whatever you used to knock poor Whitney on the head. The doctor might need to see it."

Victoria Paderevsky was speechless—possibly, Whitney thought, for the first time in her life. Daniel looked downright pleased with himself. "Did you forget what you hit her with—or did you lose it?" he asked, rubbing it in. "Tut-

tut. Well, come along, ladies. We've lots to do this afternoon. You *are* coming, aren't you, Paddie?"

She grimaced and followed him out the door.

Whitney snuggled up against Daniel's chest and enjoyed
the ride.

Two hours later Whitney was stretched out on the settee
on Daniel's front porch humming the first movement of
Mozart's Horn Concerto No. 3 and wondering why she was
in such a good mood. By most definitions, it had not been a
sterling twenty-four hours. As she had predicted, however,
she didn't have a concussion. Daniel had prevailed and
taken her to the emergency room at an Orlando hospital.
Paddie had been remarkably quiet, but Whitney assumed
she was only trying to manufacture some tale for Daniel's
consumption. Whitney couldn't imagine why Paddie would
want to tell her chairman of the board she had suspected
him of kidnapping a French horn player. But did she still
believe Harry had been kidnapped?

Daniel had moved to carry Whitney into the hospital,
but she had regained full use of her faculties and had decided he was quite bossy enough without her acting like
some helpless damsel. She would walk. It wasn't as much
fun, but she had an image to maintain.

The doctor gave her sample prescriptions of a painkiller
and some enzyme to promote healing and said she had a
bruise on the back of her neck. He suggested she rest and
stay calm. Whitney had begun to laugh somewhat hysteri-
cally, but Daniel had dragged her off before the doctor
could recommend a padded cell. Rest and stay calm! With
Daniel Graham in her life? And Victoria Paderevsky?

Daniel had grabbed Paddie out of the waiting room,
where she was lecturing a baffled adolescent boy on Beethoven and the transition to nineteenth-century Romanti-
cism. The boy was obviously glad to see her go.

When they reached the tan stucco house amid the endless acres of citrus groves, Whitney had told Daniel she
was starving and would shrivel up and die within the hour
if she didn't get something to eat; the toast and marmalade
of this morning were long gone. "Some of that Gouda
cheese in the fridge would be nice," she suggested, "and a
pot of Earl Grey tea."

"I don't have any Earl Grey tea."

"Yes, you do—in the pantry, top shelf."

Muttering something about thieves and a man's privacy, he had tossed his suit coat on the wicker chair and gone inside. As soon as the screen door shut, Whitney sat up straight and prepared to consult with Paddie on what they were and were not going to tell their handsome host— and what had happened back at the auditorium.

But then he had burst through the door and snapped his fingers at Paddie. "Paddie, you come with me," he commanded. "I don't want you two conspiring while I'm gone."

Paddie had given Whitney a dirty look, as though his use of her forbidden nickname and everything else were Whitney's fault, and followed Daniel inside.

And Whitney had begun humming Mozart.

She should be *playing* Mozart, she thought. Harry would be disgusted, she thought. He wouldn't care that she was in an unaccountably good mood while he could be languishing in some sweatbox. She had hardly touched her horn in two days. *That* would infuriate him. Murder and mayhem and handsome men weren't supposed to impede one's practice hours.

Ah, she thought, starting in on the Romanza movement, but Daniel Graham was handsome, wasn't he?

He and Paddie returned with a tray each of tea, sandwiches, and a sleeve of Fig Newtons and set them on the table next to the settee.

"For a rich man," Paddie said, plopping into an old pine rocking chair, "his kitchen leaves much to be desired."

"Yes, I know," Whitney replied.

Daniel gave her a dark look. She smiled and snatched a ham and Gouda cheese sandwich.

"All right," Daniel said as he sat down, "talk."

Paddie and Whitney just looked at him.

"I can see this is going to be a long night," he commented dryly. "Look, I have a pretty good idea of what you two have been up to and why. You think I had something to do with Harry's leaving town. Maybe you think I killed him or drove him off, I don't know. But—"

Paddie humphed. "Where did you get such a fantastic idea? You could write operas. Mr. Stagliatti resigned his position and left Orlando. I have his letter."

With barely restrained impatience, Daniel snapped up, grabbed a Fig Newton, and, biting it in half, sat down again. Whitney observed the thickness of his thighs and the flatness of his abdomen and even the muscles in his jaw as he chewed. She would let Paddie field his questions. Obviously the bump on Whitney's head had scrambled her brains.

"And you believe that?" he asked sharply.

"I do."

"Whitney?"

He fastened his sea-green eyes on her; she swallowed a mouthful of sandwich. "I wasn't here."

"But you're his student. Would he walk out like this?"

"You never know with Harry."

"Doesn't it concern you that he said he'd be gone a couple of days and he's been gone four?"

Yes, Whitney thought, but managed a shrug. "I'll start worrying if he's not back by Monday."

"What does he think of Paddie?"

"Same as everyone else—that she's a tyrant with a rare musical gift."

"He should talk," Paddie muttered. Whitney was surprised; Paddie never muttered.

"Fine," Daniel went on impatiently, loosening his tie. "But would he walk out on her?"

Whitney caught a chunk of cheese as it fell out from between the slices of whole wheat bread. "Permanently, you mean? I don't know. He might." She stuffed the cheese back into her sandwich.

Daniel tugged off his tie and said offhandedly, "Then you don't think he was murdered or kidnapped?"

"Murdered! Kidnapped! Of course not."

Paddie winced. Daniel scowled. "Whitney," he said, "remember what I said about your ability to lie?"

Whitney didn't answer, instead laying her sandwich on the tray and pouring herself a cup of tea. She added a healthy dollop of cream. Daniel was unbuttoning his cuffs. She noticed the grim set of his mouth, the fine, tanned muscles of his hands, the dark hairs on his wrists.

"Paddie put you up to breaking into my office yesterday, didn't she?" Daniel went on. "You've been covering for her, Whitney. If not because you think your horn teacher's in danger, then why?"

"Imagine the operas this man could write," Paddie said, coming to Whitney's rescue. "You do the libretto, Daniel, and I'll do the score."

Daniel ignored her, gazing steadily at Whitney.

"I have a sense of loyalty, Daniel," she said, picking up her sandwich. "A confidence is a confidence."

"Meaning Paddie talked you into breaking into my office, camping in my grove, and searching my house, and you don't intend to tell me why."

Whitney glanced over at Paddie, who was chewing on a hunk of cheese, and then back at Daniel. Being loyal to a woman she hadn't seen in eight years had its problems. But Whitney wanted Paddie to conduct and would do what she could to stand behind her and keep her reputation intact. And yet, she wondered, if Harry *was* in danger, wouldn't it be nice to have Daniel on their side? Perhaps it was foolish not to confide in him. She looked at him and lifted her shoulders, both stubborn and apologetic. She couldn't talk, not yet.

"So you won't tell me about Harry and your 'confidence' with Paddie. All right." He paused thoughtfully. "I'll let it go—for now. Let's discuss your behavior this past week or so, Paddie."

Paddie's eyes opened with surprise. "My work, you mean?"

"No. I mean your behavior. You haven't been yourself, have you?"

"And who else would I be? Toscanini? Koussevitzky? Come, Daniel, be sensible."

He stretched out his long legs, calm now that he had the brilliant and elusive conductor in his pincers. "The coffee you spit all over Yoshifumi—what was in it?"

To Whitney's amazement and relief, after a fleeting moment of shock registered on her unbecoming features, Paddie admitted, "Soap."

"You're sure?"

"No. It tasted like soap."

"But you've no proof."

"No."

"All right. What about the score?"

"The cover was switched. Another time one was misplaced—the Stravinsky." Paddie leaned over and poured herself a cup of tea. "I do not misplace scores."

Whitney hoped Daniel knew better than to argue with that statement. Apparently he did. He turned the cuff up on his sleeve and rolled it. "The bad nights?"

"Threatening and obscene telephone calls."

"Anything in particular?"

"Ordinary nastiness."

He turned to Whitney. "You knew all this?"

"I—yes."

"When Paddie called you to replace Harry, she told you?"

Whitney nodded.

"And you two put two and two together and came up with me as the culprit. Why?"

"You don't like me," Paddie replied, not with self-pity.

"I respect you. I assumed that was enough."

"Do you? You've never said."

"I'm saying so now."

Whitney could see Paddie's eyes light up. Camaraderie had never mattered to her. Respect had. And did. "Good," she said.

Daniel sighed and turned his attention to Whitney. "You broke into my office and searched my house for some sort of proof of my culpability, am I right?"

"Or your innocence," Whitney said.

"I see," he said tightly, and finished rolling up his sleeves.

Whitney ate the rest of her sandwich. Paddie drank her tea.

"Well, then, is there anything else?" Daniel asked finally. "Any other 'happenings'?"

"No," Paddie replied.

Whitney thought of the drawing, but supposed there was no point in mentioning it. The insult to Victoria Paderevsky it represented was too close, too grating, with the CFSO premiere just days away.

"Fine." He got up and poured himself a cup of tea. As he leaned over, Whitney could see the muscles in his back straining beneath the fine fabric of his shirt. He sat back down, mug in hand. He hadn't added a dollop of cream to his tea. "Let's discuss this morning."

"Are you going to tell Victoria about the secret meeting?" Whitney asked boldly.

"As a matter of fact," Daniel said with a cool look, "I am. Or would you prefer to? You heard everything, didn't you?"

"I was playing maid."

Daniel's eyes darkened, but Paddie wasn't about to be put off by an argument. "What secret meeting?" she demanded.

Daniel turned to Paddie and explained, maintaining he would have confronted her with this problem no matter what had or hadn't happened to Whitney. He didn't believe in secret meetings.

"My own people sneaking behind my back. Who were they?"

"That's confidential."

"And they think I'm cracking under the strain? *Me?*"

"It wouldn't be unreasonable."

"Because I am a woman they hate me! Because I am overweight! Because I am *good!* Damn them. Damn them all. I will show them."

"Paddie," Daniel said with surprising patience, "that attitude isn't going to work. You're not going to show them a damned thing. Without your orchestra, you're just another overweight, unemployed musician."

Anyone else—Whitney included—would have slapped him silly, but Paddie just laughed. "I am most egotistical when I am angry," she said.

"And hurt," Daniel added softly.

Paddie just shrugged. The man, Whitney realized, had her completely cowed.

Finally Whitney spoke up. "They weren't going against you, Victoria. They're concerned. I don't see how you can keep going with the premiere just one week away and all this happening. An artist can't hide her feelings and still be true to her art. You *are* under pressure, but for very real, tangible reasons."

"That's right," Daniel said heavily. "It looks as though someone wants to see Victoria Paderevsky take a nosedive—and it sure as hell isn't me. I ought to flog you for ever thinking such a thing, Doctor."

Paddie just looked at him placidly. Whitney wondered if she was going to ask Daniel why he'd been skulking about Harry's hotel room. That had yet to be explained.

"But whoever is after you knows Whitney's been trying to help you and attacked her today—twice. Up until now everything seems to have been carefully planned and executed so Paddie was the only one who saw or heard anything. That way we could all think she was just imagining things. But now Whitney's directly involved, too. I don't know what it means, but I don't like it."

"Neither do I," Whitney said, her head hurting. She grabbed a couple of Fig Newtons, hoping they would help.

"And, for God's sake, Paddie, don't try to tell me you're the one who hit Whitney. It just makes me more suspicious."

"I did not hit her," Paddie admitted.

"All right. We have enough to take to the police."

"No!" Paddie leaped up. "No, I will not stand for it. What can they do? Nothing. What can they tell me that I don't already know? Nothing. It would only be bad publicity for me and the orchestra. No."

"Sit down, Paddie," Daniel growled. "Whitney was hit on the head. That alone suggests this business is getting ugly."

"She was not hurt badly. Whoever hit her must not have intended to do much damage—perhaps he just wanted to scare her. He could have killed her then, if he meant to."

Daniel sighed; Whitney tried to concentrate on her Fig Newtons. "Was she hit because she's helping you," he said, "or because she's Harry's student and replacement, or because she was mistaken for you?"

"Whitney looks nothing like me."

"It wasn't an accident."

"Maybe it was just a coincidence," Whitney suggested. Daniel scoffed. "Not that line again."

Whitney ignored his skepticism and stated her case. "I could have arrived at Victoria's office right when our friend was about to plant another surprise for her. He or she had to hit me to avoid being seen."

"But Paddie was right there in the building!"

"I had just left for lunch," Paddie said. "I heard something—Whitney falling, I think—and came back."

"Alone?" Daniel raised a brow. "You're braver than I thought, Doctor, or just as foolhardy as your sidekick here."

Whitney resisted an acerbic comment. "What about you, Daniel? Why did you come back?"

"For you. I realized I was taking off with your only means of transportation. I was going to give you a ride back to the house."

Whitney was properly chastened. "Oh."

"Obviously either I or Paddie could have hit you."

"Impossible," Paddie declared.

"No, it isn't. I could have hit her and ducked into a practice room until someone had found her. And you've already tried to take the blame, Paddie. If I'd had my wits about me at all I'd have searched the area."

"Ah," Paddie said genially, "but you were worried about your Whitney."

"Yes," Daniel said, and balanced his mug on the end of his knee. "Any suggestions?"

Whitney was surprised to hear him ask their opinion. "No, but I agree with Victoria about the police," she said. "We can't have them crawling around the orchestra asking questions. People are uptight enough as it is."

His sea-green eyes met hers; they were unsmiling, grim, but tender, somehow. "We can't have you or Paddie getting killed, either."

"No one wants to kill us," Whitney said, wishing her body permitted her to feel more confident. "Someone's out to drive Victoria crazy. We know that, and we can combat it. She has allies now—us. Someone to talk to. As for me—I was bonked on the head because I was in the wrong place at the wrong time. I'll be more careful in the future."

"Whitney's right," Paddie said. "We cannot risk bringing in the police now. That would only make this loathsome individual more cautious. We would be in an even worse position than we are now."

Daniel frowned. "How do you propose to explain Whitney's bruise?"

"I will say I mistook her for a burglar. The real person

who hit her will know better, of course, but obviously won't come forward with the truth."

"Oh, come off it, Paddie, you know that won't work!"

"This time I agree with Daniel," Whitney said, "except I think we should just not mention the incident. Why bother? The lump isn't that noticeable, and I'll have the weekend to recuperate before I have to perform. The person who hit me will know, but hopefully will think we're too scared or whatever to go to the police."

Daniel shook his head. "You might as well post a notice that you and Paddie are in cahoots."

"Not necessarily. Victoria could have talked me out of reporting the incident for the sake of the orchestra."

Paddie nodded, satisfied. "There, you see? That is what I would have done, too."

"I don't like it," Daniel pronounced.

"You don't have to like it, Daniel," Whitney said with a light smile, glad he was on their side, "but it's the best deal you're going to get. Victoria isn't going to corroborate anything you say to the police, and neither am I."

"You're crazy—both of you."

"I'm sure our mysterious someone would be happy to know it," Paddie commented with a grim smile.

Daniel set his mug on the floor. "I want you both to keep a low profile," he directed. "Don't do anything suspicious—and no more break-ins, searches, nothing. Damn it, do you realize what I could have done if I *had* been your man? And I want to know *everything* that happens to either of you that is the slightest bit out of the ordinary—or out of *your* ordinary, I should say. God knows you people don't live and think like the rest of us. Paddie, if you want me to put a man out at the cottage with you, I will."

"That would only be a nuisance," she replied crisply. "I am not in any physical danger, Daniel, and I assure you one of your men isn't going to help me cope with this ridiculous psychological abuse."

"I don't know," Daniel said with a sudden, sly grin. "I know a couple of guys who could distract you—"

"Please," Paddie said, pursing her lips, but Whitney thought she was holding back a smile. "What about Whitney?"

"Don't worry about me, Victoria."

Daniel leaned back in his chair and stretched out his long, thick legs. "That's right. I'll be seeing to Whitney."

"I thought as much," Paddie muttered.

"Excuse me, Mr. Graham," Whitney said, "but *Whitney* will be seeing to Whitney."

"Wrong again, sweetheart." He gave her a magnanimous and unrepentant grin that effectively silenced her. Then, all at once, he was deadly serious. "I have a feeling whoever's been playing these mind games with Paddie is about to get into some old-fashioned country hardball. In fact, I'd say he started this afternoon. I'll be damned if I'm going to let anything happen to either of you. Now finish up your tea, ladies, and don't argue. Paddie, I'll get someone to take you back to your car. What's the matter, Whitney? If you want to get the next plane back to Schenectady, I'll arrange it."

"No, you won't," Paddie said.

"Victoria's right," Whitney said, suppressing a sudden shiver of sheer terror. Paddie could be in serious trouble—and Harry. *And me,* she thought. She smiled valiantly. "I've always wanted to do the opening to *Till Eulenspiegel.*"

"Musicians," Daniel muttered, and reached for a sandwich.

Chapter Seven

An hour later Whitney still felt like eating. Daniel had given Paddie a ride back to the auditorium to pick up her car and said he had to make an appearance at his office while he was in town. Whitney was to make herself at home. She was not, however, to talk to strangers, answer the phone, wander around in the grove, or try to take "matters" in her own hands. So she decided to cook. What she wanted was a true Stagliatti spaghetti sauce. "Cures what ails you," Harry had always said.

She was browning a pound of frozen hamburger and discovering the glories of a food processor in Daniel's kitchen when Bradley Fredericks and Yoshifumi Kamii came to the back door. Should she let them in, she wondered, or were they the Big Bad Wolf who was going to gobble her up? She shrugged and opened the door. All the fairy tales she had read had happy endings.

"Well, if it isn't Paddie's one true friend," Yoshifumi said, grinning. "How are you, kid? Ready to fill Stagliatti's shoes?"

"Just planning to do my best," she replied.

Yoshifumi introduced Bradley, who greeted her formally but without animosity. Explaining Daniel wasn't around, she led them into the kitchen. They sat at the table, and she attacked the frozen meat with a spatula. Her head hurt. She had taken some of the enzyme, but eschewed the painkiller, opting instead for aspirin. Yoshifumi said she looked beat. She agreed.

"Miss McCallie," Bradley said, "when do you expect Mr. Graham to return?"

"I don't know. Soon, I guess. He didn't say." The hamburger was sticking to the pan. It was the extra-lean variety, which Stagliatti scrupulously avoided. She added a little olive oil. "Why, what's up?"

Yoshifumi scratched his chin thoughtfully. He had the blunt nails and callused fingertips of a professional violinist. "You must have heard," he said, his Japanese accent almost unnoticeable. "Paddie's canceled her four o'clock rehearsals."

Whitney turned down the heat. "Mmm, I heard." She grinned over at the two men. "I've been waiting for the sky to fall down."

"Any idea of her motives?"

"I was under the impression she thought the orchestra was beginning to react to all the strain it's been under."

Yoshifumi laughed. Bradley looked dour. "We are not the ones reacting to the pressures," he said. "You've seen Dr. Paderevsky, haven't you? What do you think?"

"I saw her briefly. Seems like the same old Paddie to me."

"Did you tell her about our little meeting this morning?" Yoshifumi asked.

"No, why would I do that?"

"Did you listen in?"

"Certainly not!"

Yoshifumi grinned. He really was a striking man, she thought. "Then you're not the same old Whitney I know. How come you sneaked off with Graham's car?"

"I did not sneak off. I merely borrowed it."

"That's what he said, but he was pissed, believe you me."

"It was just a misunderstanding."

"I'm sure it's none of our business," Bradley said impatiently. "We won't impose on you any longer, Miss McCallie, but if you would be so kind as to tell Mr. Graham of our visit?"

"Sure."

"We'll stop by later."

"Yeah," Yoshifumi said. "You might as well warn him Matthew's fit to be tied. So's Bradley, but he doesn't know how to show it. They think Graham and Paddie have overstepped their authority. They should have discussed the change in schedule with them. Me, I don't care. I'm just glad to get rid of those four o'clock practices. And we did encourage Graham to do something about Paddie before she drove herself nuts—not to mention us. Hey, that stuff smells good. Want us to stay for supper?"

"Your days as a starving musician are over, Yoshifumi," Whitney replied with a good-natured wave of her spatula. "Out."

Yoshifumi laughed. "Guess you want to be alone with Graham, huh?"

"We'd better leave," Bradley said in his first show of good humor, "before the woman decides to serve you up in a shish kebab."

"Paddie would never forgive me," Whitney said, laughing.

They left, and she added the minced garlic and onion to her frying pan. But the sauce wouldn't be a true Stagliatti creation: Daniel Graham didn't have any fresh basil.

By the time Daniel returned at six, Whitney had the table on the porch set. She had dragged out a linen cloth, folding it in quarters so it would fit on the little table, Wedgwood china, sterling silver, and crystal wineglasses. She decided candles would be gaudy and perhaps somewhat forward. She didn't want Daniel to think she was wooing him, although she did wonder if she was. Maybe the enzymes caused hallucinations and delusions, but, for whatever reasons, Whitney couldn't get her mind off Daniel Graham.

In any case, as he pointed out at once, spaghetti was not romantic.

Miffed, Whitney started back to the kitchen. She would have flounced, but it wasn't worth the effort. "My pasta water is at a rolling boil," she announced, and yanked open the screen door.

But Daniel caught her by the waist, turned her around, and settled his hands at the base of her spine. He smiled, and immediately she wished he hadn't. Not here, not now. She didn't want to be reminded of how much she liked his smile, of what it did to her. She was supposed to be concentrating on other things—Harry and the bump on her head and what was happening to Paddie.

"Don't go off in a huff, sweetheart," he said. Suddenly

she noticed there was a distinct gleam in his eyes. "You're lots more romantic than a plate of spaghetti."

She gave him a dubious look. "What's that supposed to mean?"

"It means," he said in a low voice, "that I can't think of anywhere I'd rather be than right here with you."

She figured she ought to think of a smart retort, but couldn't—not that it mattered. Daniel wasn't giving her a chance to answer. And, she had to admit, she didn't want one. Banter was impossible with his eyes smiling into hers. She knew what he was up to. In a way, she had invited it. She smiled, and at last he brought his mouth to hers.

With maddening leisureliness, he traced her lips with his tongue, and then slowly found his way into her mouth. Every movement was deliberately thrilling. Whitney felt her weight sinking into his arms.

"I thought I'd lost you this afternoon," he breathed into her mouth, kissing her again, "and it was awful, Whitney. I'm getting used to having you around."

"Pestering you?"

He smiled, teasing her with his tongue. "Mmm, I like the way you pester me."

"Daniel . . ."

But he held her close, pressing her to him, and their kiss deepened, and with it came a sudden, absorbing heightening of her senses. She spread her fingers on his back, felt the tensed muscles beneath them, and opened her mouth wider, flicking her tongue against his teeth, feeling her breasts straining, her body responding to every nuance of his.

He brushed the line of her jaw with one finger, sending tiny shivers coursing through her, and then he skimmed her throat and, opening his hand, stopped just above her breasts.

"I don't want to rush you, Whitney," he murmured, pulling his mouth from hers.

She smiled. "But?"

He grinned, and she thought she would melt. What was it about him that drew her so unerringly? She didn't know. She didn't care. She only knew that she was there, in his arms, and could think of no place she would rather be.

"But," he said with a light smack on her behind, "I'd like nothing better than to cart you upstairs and make love to you until you couldn't see straight."

"Daniel!"

His grin broadened. "You asked, darlin'."

"So I did." She grinned back at him. "Suppose I told you I already can't see straight?"

"I'd blame the lump on your head."

"You'd be wrong."

"Would I?" He twirled a lock of her hair around one finger and let it go. "Then you have quite a time coming to you, sweets. Meanwhile, though, your pasta water's boiling."

"Oh. So it is."

They had just finished up the dishes and retired to the living room with glasses of brandy when Rebecca Graham arrived, sweeping in wearing a fresh turquoise suit and promising to stay but a minute. She was on her way to a meeting. Daniel commented that she was always on her way to a meeting, but Rebecca took the implied criticism in stride and dished out a little of her own. His maid, after all, had turned out to be a virtuoso hornist, which, she said, was just as well. Charles, her husband, would never have approved otherwise. He was at home—apparently where he preferred to be—and sent his love. Whitney had already deduced that the Grahams were a tight-knit and prominent family in Florida, willing to do their civic duty, and strong backers of the arts.

"Charles said I should keep my nose out of your affairs, but of course I can't resist," she said, sitting on the very edge of the sofa. "You're my son."

Her son, who was a corporate vice president and had strands of gray in his hair, gave her an indulgent look. Whitney sat back in her chair and sipped her brandy. She was enjoying herself.

"Mother," Daniel said, "you're here about the orchestra, aren't you?"

"You're inciting open revolt."

"That's ridiculous." The indulgent look vanished. Whitney suddenly remembered Yoshifumi's and Bradley's visit; she had forgotten to tell Daniel. He was scowling at his mother. "People came to me because they wanted action. Well, they got it. I think they're just looking for someone to be mad at. If not Paddie, then why not me? I don't care. Venting a little steam might be good for them."

Rebecca blinked. "Paddie?"

Daniel waved his fingers dismissively. "Dr. Paderevsky."

"You didn't go through proper channels, Daniel. Even Thomas Walker agrees, and you *know* he's the first to endorse expediency."

"He's just upset because I bypassed Matthew."

"My phone's been ringing all afternoon. What was a quiet matter this morning is hardly quiet now. Daniel, people think Dr. Paderevsky can't handle the strain of directing a major orchestra. The premiere is just one week away! Canceling the four o'clock rehearsals has only fueled their suspicions. I know what you were trying to do, but if you had consulted with people, they wouldn't be so shocked now."

"There wasn't time to wait for a consensus."

They argued back and forth for a few minutes. Whitney propped herself up in her chair and tried to look as if she hadn't been bonked on the head. Daniel and Rebecca didn't ask for any comments from her, so she didn't give any. Nor did she feel sorry for Daniel. He wasn't the type of man to let criticism from his mother get to him, and Whitney was quite amazed that he could keep all the little ins and outs of what had been happening the past few days straight. She would have blurted out something she shouldn't have long before now.

Finally Rebecca left, apologizing to Whitney for interrupting. Whitney just smiled.

"She seems like a nice woman," she said to Daniel when Rebecca had gone.

He just growled and got another brandy.

"Think she wants to get rid of Paddie?"

"She's the one who recommended her!" he said irritably and sat on the arm of Whitney's chair. His hip was touching her upper arm, but she made no move to alter her position. "Saw her conduct in Amsterdam and decided central Florida needed to work on its good-ol'-boy reputation. So

she decided hiring a woman for music director of the CFSO would do the trick."

"But I thought you brought Paddie to Orlando?"

"I did, curse my soul. Mother recommended her, but I got her." He grinned down at her over the top of his glass. "I saw her conduct in Amsterdam, too. We were on a business trip, and I took Mother to the symphony."

"What about Charles?"

"Father is not a fan of classical music."

"He prefers Flatt and Scruggs?"

"Infinitely."

"They must make an interesting pair." Whitney polished off the last of her brandy and wondered if it was reacting with the enzymes. She felt downright giddy. She looked at Daniel and said, "What would your father say if he'd caught you kissing a French horn player?"

"My darlin' Whitney, my father would hardly think of you as a horn player."

"But I am."

"Don't remind me, love," he teased. "You've already got enough strikes against you."

She gazed up at him, unswayed by his taunt. "Such as?"

"You're Victoria Paderevsky's 'one true friend'—"

"Yes, I can't imagine why she said that."

"I'll bet you can't. And you're Harry Stagliatti's student—"

"What's wrong with Harry?"

"He's almost as cantankerous as Paddie."

"True, but he's an incredible virtuoso. So was his father."

"I'm sure."

"What other strikes do I have against me?"

He leaned against the back of the chair and stretched his arm over Whitney's shoulder, fingering her hair. The bounce was back in her curls. She leaned back, too, nestling herself in the inside curve of his chest and shoulder. "You're a New York Yankee," he said, a twinge of humor in his deep drawl. "My parents fancy me hooking up with another old Florida citrus family—the Walkers, for instance. They don't own anywhere near as many acres as we do, but they've been in this area as many generations as the Grahams have."

"I don't like Thomas Walker."

"He does have his prejudices, to be sure, but, as I say, he's been around for a long time."

"Matthew seems charming, though."

"Yes," Daniel said, "that's always been one of his better qualities—and not always appreciated."

"Are you two friends?"

"Matt and I? We go back a long ways—I've tried to help him along. He's a natural as general manager, but I'm not sure it's something he wants to do for the rest of his life. But I don't know anyone else who could stand working that closely with our Victoria Paderevsky."

"The Walkers and the Grahams seem to have a lot at stake with the CFSO," Whitney said softly, thinking how much Paddie had at stake.

"More than some other people on the board, perhaps, but the community support for the orchestra has been unbelievable—and we all want to make it work. Central Florida is getting national and international attention out of this. Naturally we want it to be favorable attention. And Matt's the only one of us who actually works for the orchestra."

"Did you get him the job? I can't see Thomas pulling any strings for his son to work with Paddie."

Daniel laughed, but said seriously, "Matt got the job on his own merits. However—as I was saying—he has a twenty-year-old sister at the University of Florida . . ."

"Uh-oh, there's another strike against me. I'm twenty-nine."

"A regular old lady."

"I was never a cheerleader."

"Played horn in a marching band?"

"Heaven forbid."

Daniel laughed softly. "Father will never approve." And when she looked up, surprise and fear in her expression, she saw that the laughter had reached his eyes. "Of course," he went on in a languorous, seductive voice, "one look at your big blue eyes and he'll be hopelessly smitten . . . just like me. Well, not exactly."

"Daniel, Daniel . . ." She polished off the last of her brandy and grinned up at him. "I can imagine what you must have been thinking about me all this time, but I—"

She hesitated, then blurted out, "I never did believe you
had Harry chained to a grapefruit tree or something."

Daniel's eyes narrowed suspiciously. "I see. I thought,
Whitney, that you believed his letter." He finished his
brandy and set the empty glass on the antique marble
table at his side. "Don't you?"

Whitney realized her mistake too late. "Yes, yes, I do."

"But?"

"But I thought— Well, your questions *have* made me
wonder. You *don't*, do you?"

"Have Harry chained to a grapefruit tree? No."

He gave Whitney a look that prompted her to wonder if
she were more eccentric than she thought she was. Then
he sighed heavily. And then he burst out laughing.

Whitney realized she probably shouldn't have mentioned Harry, but he was on her mind. She *had* to find out
what he was up to! If only he'd called and told her before
he'd made his exit. And she wished she understood why
Paddie hadn't just come right out and asked about Daniel
being in Harry's hotel room. Did that mean Paddie still believed him somehow responsible for Harry's exit—or was
she just trying to protect her reputation? She'd jumped to
enough bizarre conclusions as it was. Still, it made no
sense. Paddie had to know Daniel was on their side! But, of
course, they were dealing with a woman who memorized
entire symphonic scores. Paddie simply didn't think like
other people.

Whitney started to tell Daniel about Bradley's and
Yoshifumi's visit, but there was a knock at the back door.
And then another. The place began filling up with people.
First Thomas Walker arrived, immediately alienating
Whitney by suggesting that Daniel should have fired that
"fat ugly witch" instead of accommodating her. Apparently he felt he could speak his mind in front of Daniel. He
also muttered to Whitney, as though she would quite naturally agree with him, that he didn't trust people of Paddie's "national origin." Whitney calmly pointed out that
her national origin was Brooklyn, New York. Thomas
nodded in agreement as though Brooklyn was in Outer
Mongolia.

Bradley, Yoshifumi, and Matthew Walker arrived next.
Matthew greeted Whitney graciously, but didn't look too

pleased to see his father. She could hardly blame him. Matthew was charming. Thomas was odious. Then Angelina Carter and the lanky black man, who was indeed cellist Lucas Washington, joined the group. Whitney managed to keep from smirking when Lucas sat next to Thomas on the sofa, slapped his knees, and said, "Hey, how're you doing, Tom?" Lucas was obviously well aware of the older Walker's prejudices.

Everyone wanted to know what Daniel had said and done to Paddie for her to cancel a rehearsal and rearrange her schedule, which, for all intents and purposes, she had carved in stone. Was this another sign of her cracking up?

No, Daniel said; he and Paddie—he referred to her as Dr. Paderevsky in front of everyone else—had had a long, frank talk. He maintained she had been worried about the orchestra's reaction to Harry Stagliatti's insensitivity and unprofessional behavior, and the strain they'd all been under. She'd been working them hard. Yes, she did admit she hadn't been herself the past few days—because of Harry and because of her concerns for the mental well-being of her orchestra. Daniel said he had suggested canceling that afternoon's rehearsal, and Paddie agreed; then went a step further and recommended a permanent change in the rehearsal schedule. And they all bought every word of it. Whitney was amazed. They'd been working with the woman for weeks and they didn't realize she would *never* let her work be affected by mere worry and certainly wouldn't admit it if she had. Daniel Graham, she realized, was that slick. Even Matthew Walker and Bradley Fredericks, who were supposed to be so angry, didn't argue.

"I wish I'd been informed sooner," Matthew said, rather magnanimously, Whitney thought, "but maybe this will do the trick."

There were numerous murmurings of "I hope so."

Angelina peered at Whitney. "You look pretty tired, Whit."

"It's been a long day," she said in a glorious understatement.

"Don't worry," Thomas Walker said heartily. "A few days in the Florida sun will cure those Rust Belt miseries of yours."

Whitney gritted her teeth.

"You'd better rest up," Angelina suggested seriously. "Harry's been playing his ass off for Paddie. Don't think she won't expect the same from you."

"Is there any resentment among the other horns about me coming in like this?"

"Are you kidding?" This was from Lucas. "They figure you're Joan of Arc come to save them. They're smart enough not to want to launch the CFSO with that bitch of a solo."

Whitney knew he was referring to *Till Eulenspiegel*. "I guess I'm not that smart," Whitney said dryly.

"No," Lucas said, "you're that good."

"Trust us, Whitney," Matthew Walker reassured her. "Dr. Paderevsky wouldn't have hired you if you couldn't measure up to Harry."

"I hope I won't have to," she said. "I'm counting on him being back by opening night."

"If Dr. Paderevsky will have him," Matthew said.

Whitney decided she liked Matthew Walker and Lucas Washington. She had always liked Yoshifumi and Angelina. She despised Thomas Walker, who seemed to have no respect for anyone, including his own son. The jury was still out on Bradley. He didn't say much. Then they all started talking music, and Bradley joined right in. He absolutely rhapsodized about the orchestra—not about Paddie, although he wasn't as openly critical as the others, but about the CFSO itself. It was going to be world-class, he said; there was no doubt about it. Whitney decided she liked him, too.

They were discussing current orchestral recordings when the brakes of a car screeched in the driveway. Daniel, who had been looking bored, leaped up.

But he was too late to cut Paddie off at the kitchen. She came storming into the elegant living room. Her hair was sticking out everywhere. Her eyes were wild. Her black stretch knit pants had holes in the knees. She was carrying a long stick.

And on the end of it was a rattlesnake.

"I have had enough!" she shrieked.

Then she dumped the thing on the floor.

Angelina screamed. Yoshifumi started babbling in Japanese. Matthew and Bradley turned white. Thomas assured them all the snake was dead. Lucas stretched out his interminable legs and started to laugh.

Daniel snatched the stick out of Paddie's hand. "For the love of Jesus, Paddie," he snarled, and removed the snake from both the polite and the impolite company.

Whitney just stared at Paddie. Her shoulders were heaving. Her face was purple. In the chair beside Whitney, Angelina suggested someone call a doctor. No one moved.

Paddie sucked in a deep breath and pointed a finger at the group. "A head doctor, is that what you think I need?" she bellowed. "Ha! What would you do if you found a snake in your living room? You all— I promise you, I will find out who is doing this to me." She paused, her breathing labored; everyone stared. "This time you have gone too far."

It was Thomas Walker who got up and led Paddie to a chair. "Now you listen to me, Dr. Paderevsky," he said, putting a comforting arm around her shoulder. "This wasn't anyone's doing. Florida is full of rattlesnakes, and your cottage is in the country. A snake could easily get into your living room. Did you kill it yourself?"

"Who else do you think would? I can take care of myself!"

"Of course you can."

Thomas cajoled her as if she were a five-year-old. Whitney started to like him better, but then she realized that Paddie had just become something familiar to him: a woman afraid of snakes. He hadn't noticed at all that Paddie wasn't afraid or even particularly distraught. She was seething, so angry she was very nearly inarticulate.

Daniel returned and curtly ordered everyone out. Thomas didn't think that included him, but Daniel made it clear it did. So he left with the others.

Whitney went and sat on the sofa next to Paddie. Daniel loomed above them, pacing furiously. Whitney scowled up at him. "You could show a little more compassion, you know."

But he just glared at Paddie. "All right, Dr. Paderevsky," he said. "Where did you get it?"

She sniffed, suddenly in control of herself. "The snake you mean?"

"Yes, damn it, I mean the snake!"

Whitney leaped to Paddie's defense. "Daniel, you're hardly being fair—"

"I'm not, am I?" Now he glared at Whitney, too. "Well, Paddie, shall you tell her or shall I?"

Paddie sat up straight and said in her fake Lithuanian accent, "I do not know what you are talking about."

"I am talking about your goddamn snake that's been dead over a week!"

Chapter Eight

PADDIE didn't look the least bit chastened by Daniel's fury. "How could you tell?" she asked curiously.

"I'm not stupid."

Reluctantly, Whitney began to realize what had happened. She glanced up at Daniel. Clearly he was in a black mood. He paced across the Oriental carpet, occasionally raking his fingers through his hair and growling. And he had been so genial through dinner, Whitney thought. They had discussed Graham Citrus—it was a bigger corporation than she had imagined—and the effects of central Florida's phenomenal growth on the citrus industry. He had told her hair-raising stories about alligators, but promised there were none in his lake. By a mutual but unspoken agreement they hadn't discussed Paddie's plight.

Whitney glanced over at Paddie. Clearly she didn't care if Daniel was in a black mood. She was looking sanctimonious.

"Victoria," Whitney said reprovingly, "you didn't."

Paddie folded her arms over her ample chest. "It was necessary."

"To what end?" Daniel demanded.

"We were at a stalemate, this filth and I." Paddie was using her Lithuanian accent again: expostulating. "I wanted to draw him out. I came upon the snake on my night walk in the grove and chose to make him the centerpiece of my plan."

Daniel regarded her with profound disbelief. "Your plan," he repeated in a dangerous monotone.

"Yes," Paddie said placidly.

Whitney wanted to take Daniel's hand and calm him

down, but he looked as unapproachable as a rhinoceros on a rampage. She was suitably impressed, but Paddie was not. She asked Whitney for a drink of water; all that trembling had dried her throat.

This was too much for Daniel. He spun around and bellowed, *"Get your own goddamn drink of water!"*

"Ah, yes," Paddie said, "I forgot about your bump."

And she got up and went into the kitchen. Daniel glared at Whitney. "That woman is your friend?"

"I haven't seen her in eight years."

"And yet you were willing to risk breaking into my office on her behalf?"

And Harry's, Whitney thought. "Women musicians have to stick together."

"I could have had you arrested."

"But you didn't."

"Maybe I should have! You realize, don't you, that when you and I were at odds she would never have come forward to protect you?"

"I know," Whitney said.

"And yet you protected her?"

"I kept my promises."

"Knowing she wouldn't have done the same for you?"

"I don't judge people on the basis of what they'll do for me," she replied coolly.

Paddie returned and, with a profound sigh of satisfaction, settled into a wingback chair. "Much better," she said. "Daniel, sit down and relax. What's done is done."

Whitney observed he was no longer Mr. Graham. Had she missed something along the way? Did Paddie actually consider this man a friend? Stranger things had happened in the life of Victoria Paderevsky, to be sure, but few more unexpected.

"I believe one of the people in this room tonight is the miserable scorpion who has been harassing me," she explained calmly. "I knew they would come, of course."

Daniel wasn't letting anything slip by. "How?"

"I know my musicians." She glanced up at Daniel, as if daring him to argue. He didn't. "They were the same ones who came to see you this morning, were they not? I know you won't answer. You are too much of a businessman and a gentleman. In your position, I would have handed me a list of all their names. In any case, I wanted to see what kind of reaction I would get. They all think I'm crazy anyway, don't they?"

"Apparently not without reason."

"I am immune to your sarcasm, Daniel."

"Well," he said, "did you discover anything?"

"Lucas Washington has a perverse sense of humor."

Daniel's mouth twisted to one side, and with some surprise Whitney realized he was trying to keep from laughing. He was a man of abrupt and varied moods, but at least, she thought, one knew where one stood with him— sometimes all too clearly.

Paddie didn't notice his amusement. "Other than that," she said gravely, "I learned nothing."

"Victoria," Whitney said, "whoever's been harassing you knew he didn't sic a rattlesnake on you."

"That's right," Daniel said, recovered now. "What did you expect him to do? Stand up and say, 'I didn't do it, I didn't do it'?"

Daniel's imitation of a sissy was remarkable. Whitney tried not to laugh.

Paddie scoffed. "Of course not. But he is on the defensive now, isn't he?"

Daniel shook his head in exasperation. "I think all your theatrics have gone for naught, Paddie."

"Yes, well." She shrugged and drained her glass of water. "We shall see."

Whitney saw Paddie to the door. Outside the night was quiet and cool. Whitney breathed in the scent of the groves. "It's beautiful here," she said, sighing. "Even with all this going on, I can't help but be glad I'm not in Schenectady right now."

"That wouldn't have anything to do with Daniel Graham, would it?" Paddie asked.

"I hardly know the man."

"True," Paddie said, getting into her car, "but you have always been sentimental. You cry at operas instead of analyzing the music. In operas, there is often love at first sight, is there not?"

"And tragic endings."

Paddie grinned; she almost looked attractive. "That is why real life is so wonderful." She patted Whitney's hand.

"We will find Harry, and we will end all this nonsense. Then this man of yours can romance you properly—if he can wait that long."

"Victoria, he isn't—"

"He is, Whitney," Paddie interrupted. "And so are you."

Whitney could think of nothing to say. Paddie promised there would be no more snakes, said she was glad Whitney had proved herself worthy of Harry Stagliatti's seat in the orchestra by not fainting at the sight of a snake, and drove off.

At midnight Whitney was still unable to sleep. She was sitting up in bed doing deep-breathing exercises and trying not to think about all the things troubling her. Paddie. Harry. Daniel. She wanted to believe everything would be all right, but didn't dare. She wanted Paddie to conduct. She wanted Harry to contact her or Paddie or someone in the orchestra and tell them what he was up to. What if something *had* happened to him? She didn't think she could go on. He *had* to be all right.

And Daniel. He confused and excited her and occupied a place in her thoughts that no one else ever had, not really, not this way. She had known him little over a day. It *was* like an opera. And was he a Don Giovanni? A Faust? After all, what did she know about Daniel Graham? And how dare she let him seep into her consciousness, into her very being! Harry could be kidnapped or dead or dying and she was lusting after a man she hardly knew!

No, not lusting . . .

Yes, lusting. That was part of the problem. And yet it was more than lusting, and that was the other part of the problem.

The door to her bedroom silently opened.

She exhaled very, very slowly. Now what? After seeing Paddie off, she'd come inside and, finding the living room empty, had walked out onto the porch. Daniel had been standing on the edge of the lake, his silhouette tall and dark against the glistening water. Somehow he had seemed even more unapproachable than he had been earlier when he'd been so furious with Paddie. Whitney had wanted to know what he was thinking and feeling. She had wanted to go to him. Instead she had gone quietly back inside, taken a warm bath, and headed for bed. For a while she had listened, waiting, for his footsteps in the hall. But they never came, and she had tried to sleep.

Now she sat motionless, not knowing what to expect, or even if she should be afraid.

Then Daniel poked his head in through the crack in the door. Whitney breathed, relieved. She hadn't realized how tensed and afraid she'd been.

"Did I scare you?" he said. "Sorry. I thought you'd be asleep by now."

She smiled. "No such luck."

"Are you hurting?"

"Not too badly, no. Just wired, mostly. I'm not used to being attacked. And I'm not used to going two days without practicing. Harry says after five days my lips'll turn black and fall off."

Daniel laughed softly as he entered the bedroom. A small lamp on the nightstand provided the only light. "They never have, have they?"

"I wouldn't know."

"You mean you've never gone five days without practicing?"

"Not since I started taking horn seriously."

He moved toward the bed. For such a big man, he was surprisingly lithe and lean, a man of physical action, yet of grace, too. She admired the fluidity of his movements and felt herself beginning to respond to him already. He sat on the edge of the bed. "What about vacations?" he asked.

Whitney was leaning against the cherry headboard. With each breath, she could feel her breasts rising and falling under her sturdy blue nightgown. Daniel had that kind of impact on her. She found herself wishing she had worn something sexier and more alluring than cotton broadcloth. Would he prefer frills? She checked her thoughts. They were discussing horn. "I bring along my horn," she explained, wondering at the hoarse timbre of her voice and the subtle, poignant ache that was spreading through her, "and get in an hour a day, minimum."

"What about sickness?"

"I've never been sick more than three days—at least not sick enough to miss practice."

He smiled: a gentle, easy smile that made her body tense, not with fear or foreboding, but with a physical attraction that was so strong it was nearly palpable. Imagining his smile was one of the things that had driven off sleep. With her eyes shut, she could see the flash of his even teeth and the glint of amusement in his sea-green eyes. Even when he wasn't near her, he was capable of stirring her emotions, and her body, in ways that made her long to be touched.

"You're compulsive, aren't you?" he drawled silkily, as though they were discussing something much more intimate than her practice schedule. "I suppose you have to be."

He was sitting very close to her, but they weren't touching. She thought it would be easier if they were. Less distracting, in a way. Then again, maybe it wouldn't be. Touching him wasn't distracting. It simply blotted all other thoughts completely from her mind.

"Most musicians are," she replied absently.

"So I've noticed."

He smiled again. Whitney sat up straighter, her back flat against the headboard. She was too tired and shaken to trust herself completely. Her instincts, she thought, could be hopelessly inaccurate tonight. And yet they were telling her more loudly, more certainly, than they had ever told her anything before that this was a man she could trust. And trust not just with her life, but with her soul. He wouldn't seize them. He wouldn't take them from her and try to control them. Tonight, with the warm spring breeze and the smell of flowers blowing in through the screens, with the shadows and the dim light softening the hard lines of his face, Daniel Graham seemed not at all threatening or domineering, but pensive and kind.

"Did you have a nice walk?" she asked, trying to divert her inappropriate thoughts.

"No. I kept thinking about you."

She tried a laugh; it wasn't very successful. "Is that good or bad?"

"I don't know." He straightened up, his voice deepening, as if he'd suddenly decided he had to be less open. But there was a tenderness in his eyes that belied the gruffness of his words. "I didn't come here to make love to you, Whitney."

"So I assumed," she said levelly, "since you thought I was asleep."

"Whitney, Whitney." He sighed, more irritated with himself now, she thought, than with her. "Whitney—you and Paddie are worried about Harry, aren't you? I *know* you are. Damn it, I wish you two would—" He broke off, but when he resumed, his voice was steady. "No, that's not fair. I know you won't say, and I understand. I appreciate your loyalties. Whitney, just remember: I have my loyalties, too."

"What are you saying?" she asked sharply, grabbing his arm. "Daniel, *has* something happened to Harry? Do you know—"

"Please, Whitney, don't." His eyes were tender, pleading, and yet, under her fingertips, his arm was tensed. "All I'm saying is that I know you haven't told me everything and I'm assuming you know I haven't told you everything."

Harry, she thought: Daniel knew she hadn't told him everything about Harry.

"But, Daniel—"

"Frustrating, isn't it, when someone won't talk?" He lifted her hand, kissed her knuckles, and held it firmly in his. Then he smiled cheerfully, changing his mood entirely, and she had to admire his willpower. "Did you hear the phone ring?"

Whitney couldn't shift moods that easily, but she nodded. Just after she'd gone to bed she'd heard the telephone.

"That was my mother."

"Ah, the gracious Rebecca Graham. She doesn't have a cottage somewhere amid the groves, too, does she?"

He grinned. "Hardly, darlin'. My parents have the big house down at the groves south of here. This is my Uncle Jesse's old place."

The big house? "Oh."

"My charming mother called to tell me she thinks you're adorable."

That and the play of his fingertips in her palm were just the distractions Whitney needed. She grimaced at his mother's comment, but relished the feel of his warm hand on hers. "And what did you say?"

"I said I quite agreed."

"You were just joking, I hope."

He laughed. "What's wrong? You don't want to be adorable?"

"When I was five, yes."

"At twenty-nine, however, one prefers to be scintillating and sexy and captivating, right?"

"Absolutely." She gave him her most fetching smile, hoping she didn't look adorable.

"Good, because those are all on the list of my first impressions of Whitney McCallie." He grinned and added, "Along with adorable, of course."

"Liar," she said, teasing, relaxing. "You thought I was a thief, remember?"

"Mmm. A scintillating, sexy, captivating, adorable thief in sweat pants and a Buffalo Sabres shirt." He let go of her hand and ran two fingers up her bare forearm. "And pink ballet slippers."

His hip touched her thigh through the covers, sending waves of warmth undulating through her. His two fingers trailed across the cotton flannel blanket on her lap and paused, slowly, absently drawing little circles on her stomach.

"I come at you waving a gun and doing my damnedest to intimidate the hell out of you and all I get are lies and indignation," he said quietly. "And here I am now, dying to kiss you, and you're nervous—"

"I am not nervous," she said.

He grinned broadly. "Good."

The hand on her stomach eased down to her side, his palm resting on the bed, and he leaned over her, bringing his face flush to hers. Her back slid down some from the headboard. Maintaining a rigid posture with him this close was more than she could manage. And she didn't want to. She wasn't nervous, not with him. She touched his cheek.

"Lovely Whitney," he said, and kissed her.

Purposefully, she slid farther down from the headboard, into his arms. Her lips parted, her tongue circling his, tasting his mouth, and she could feel the excitement growing in him as it was in her. With her body she told him this was what she wanted, what she had been waiting for, however vaguely and unknowingly.

"Darlin'," he drawled lazily, "if I knew for sure it wouldn't put you in the hospital, there's no way you could get rid of me tonight."

"I don't want to get rid of you," she said.

"I know, love, but I'm an honorable Southern gentleman, and we don't 'force' ourselves on injured women." He grinned wickedly. "No matter how much they want us to—and, of course, no matter how much we want to."

"I suppose you're right."

"Of course I'm right. The doctor said you need to stay calm, and, darlin', a night with me will be anything but calm." He leaned over once more, dragging his tongue erotically across her mouth, tantalizing her again. "But we will have that night, Whitney. I promise you that."

He propped her up against the headboard and touched her hair just above her ear. The shadows played in his eyes. With a smile filled with tenderness, he bent over and planted a kiss on her forehead. "Night-night, love."

Then he grinned and hopped off the bed.

"Daniel . . ."

He stopped halfway to the door and turned. "Here I am trying to be noble as hell and the woman is delaying me," he said with a small grin. "You're playing with fire, darlin'."

"Seems to be a bad habit with me," she said with a gentle, mocking smile. She tugged the blanket up under her chin so she wouldn't have to see the lingering physical effects of his touch. There was nothing she could do about the emotional ones. "I just wanted to tell you—I trust you, Daniel. I want you to know that."

"Go to sleep, Whitney," he said, and flicked the switch next to the door.

"Psst . . . Whitney . . . psst . . ." There was a tapping sound. "Whitney, wake up."

Wide awake, Whitney kept both eyes shut and didn't move, stifling an urge to bolt up and run.

Someone was outside her window, tapping on her screen.

If she pretended to be asleep, maybe he would go away. "It's Victoria . . ."

Now she bolted up. *"Victoria!"*

"No, shh!" came the insistent whisper.

Whitney threw off her blanket and went to the screen, silently thanking the gods that Daniel hadn't made up his mind to stay the night. Paddie was crouched next to the azalea. The soft light of dawn was streaking across the sky. Birds pranced and chirped on the lawn.

"Victoria, what is it?" Whitney whispered. "Is something wrong?"

"I don't know. You must come with me."

"Now? I don't see how—"

"Hurry! Meet me at the lake."

"Victoria, wait!"

But she was already slinking off across the dew-soaked lawn. Whitney groaned and decided whoever was trying to drive Paddie nuts had succeeded. Without bothering to get dressed, she tiptoed out the front door and ran across the lawn in her nightgown and bare feet.

Paddie was waiting under a giant cypress tree, the trunk blocking a view of her stout figure from anyone looking on from the stately house. "Did Graham hear you?" Her voice was just above a whisper.

Whitney shook her head. "What is it now?"

"I heard shots."

Paddie paused dramatically for Whitney to absorb the impact of her words and turn properly pale.

"In the grove," she went on, "toward the highway, although it was difficult to tell."

"You're sure?"

"Of course."

"Do you think . . ." Whitney swallowed hard. "Harry—oh, Paddie, do you think it's him? If he's been shot . . ."

Paddie sank against the thick trunk of the tree. She had on a clean pair of black stretch knit pants and a red sweatshirt and had washed her hair, but had not gotten around to combing it. Her tiny eyes were alive with anger and determination and something else. Fear?

Fear for Harry Stagliatti?

Whitney shook off the thought. There had to be another explanation. Poachers?

"I don't know," Paddie admitted. "But we must investigate."

Whitney shook her head, adamant. "No, not we, Victoria. This has gone too far. We have to call the police."

"And tell them what?" Paddie demanded.

"That you heard shots. That's enough. Daniel said he's had trouble with poachers. Maybe—"

"We're wasting precious time arguing—and we could waste more time contacting the police. They would be slow; they would ask too many questions. We must act *now,* Whitney. It's almost a mile's walk to my cottage."

"I'll get Daniel—"

"No!"

Whitney had already started off toward the house, but now she turned and stared, white-faced, at Paddie. "Victoria, you can't possibly still believe he's behind all this!"

"I don't know what to believe," Paddie replied, haughty despite her own uncertainty. "But I know I will not risk Harry's life. I trust you, Whitney, and only you."

"But . . ."

"Come."

"Don't you think I ought to get dressed first?"

Paddie groaned impatiently but relented, needlessly warning Whitney to be quiet.

Whitney raced back into the house, not daring even to turn on a light as she peeled off her nightgown and put on a pair of jeans, sneakers, and her sweatshirt with the bust of Beethoven silkscreened on the front. Then, silently, she tiptoed up the stairs to Daniel's room. She wouldn't disturb him. She just wanted to know he was there, safe and asleep.

But he wasn't.

His bed was empty, still neatly made, as it had been that morning. His tan suit and yellow shirt were tossed over the pillows. Whitney held her breath. Her head began to pound. Over and over again her mind said *no, no, no!*

She ran downstairs. It no longer mattered how much noise she made now, so she didn't care. She went to the gun closet in the cypress-paneled study. The key was in the lock. And why not? The two rifles that had been there that morning were gone.

But the revolver wasn't. She picked it up and felt her

stomach flip-flop. She hated guns. She didn't even know how to use one.

"I'll figure it out if I have to," she said to herself, her voice, like the rest of her, trembling.

Chapter Nine

THEY followed the path around the lake to Paddie's cottage and, refusing to discuss alternatives or turn back, ventured into the isolated section of groves west of the cottage, staying on a well-traveled sandy road that seemed to cut through the heart of the grove. Picking was being done here. Valencias, Paddie said.

They heard no shots, and saw no sign of Daniel Graham, Harry Stagliatti, or poachers.

Finally they came to a crossroads. Paddie wanted to turn left. Whitney, uncertain, looked to her right, and spotted a huge trailer truck, a monolithic silhouette in the pale light of dawn. She touched Paddie on the shoulder and pointed.

It was Paddie who spotted the pickup truck. "See," she whispered, "behind the trailer."

Whitney saw. Its bed was loaded with boxes of fruit. Poachers.

Discussion was unnecessary. They knew what they had to do. Paddie had heard shots, and poachers wouldn't be shooting at each other. Leaving the road, they crept into the grove, hiding in the cover of the older trees, their branches weighted down with tangy-smelling fruit. Paddie had grabbed her fireplace poker at the cottage and now held it high. Whitney straightened her grip on the revolver.

As they moved closer to the trailer, they could hear voices. Men's voices, their words unintelligible. Whitney listened hard for Daniel's sonorous drawl, not certain she wanted to hear it. It could mean he was in trouble . . . or causing trouble. She would have liked to stop and listen

116

and think, but Paddie ducked under the next branch and Whitney followed.

An orange dropped with a thud from a heavily laden branch.

The two women stood motionless. Whitney was grateful for the breath control she had developed after all her years playing horn. They didn't make another sound.

But nothing happened. Either the men up ahead hadn't heard the orange or had thought nothing of it. Paddie, sticking her hand behind her back, motioned for Whitney to proceed.

They ducked silently under another branch and were at the trailer, huddled along its long wooden side, the tires blocking a view of their feet from the side the voices seemed to be coming from.

"If we kill him," a man was saying disinterestedly, "it'd be cold-blooded, premeditated murder. That's not what we're being paid to do."

"He's seen us."

"So?"

"So he can describe us!"

"Big deal. He tells the cops he came across two guys stealing oranges. The cops take down the descriptions and file them. The police aren't going to catch us. But if we leave them a corpse to find—"

"They don't have to find his body. I can get rid of it."

"Yeah, well."

"Maybe we ought to check in and—"

"—and be pegged as a couple of turkeys? Forget it."

"We have to do something."

They continued arguing back and forth. Paddie and Whitney looked at each other. Someone was at the mercy of two poachers. Daniel? Impossible, Whitney thought; the man was armed to the teeth! Harry?

Whitney looked at Paddie, but the stout and brilliant conductor needed no persuading. With her mouth set grimly and her poker held firmly, she crept around the back of the trailer. Whitney nodded to herself and followed.

"If you hadn't shot the poor slob we wouldn't be in this mess," one man was saying.

"If you'd kept your voice down like I told you— Wait, did you hear something?"

"Naw. You're just getting nervous. I say we get out of here while the getting's good."

Paddie peeked around the corner of the trailer and immediately turned back to Whitney. "Harry?" Whitney mouthed.

Paddie nodded, her face white.

Whitney could feel the blood draining out of her own face, but she steadied herself, placing a hand on the trailer. *Harry Stagliatti had been shot!* Now, of all times, she couldn't fail him. She had to think clearly. She had to reason. She had to get him out of there!

Paddie held up two fingers. Then she held up one finger. Two men. One gun.

Whitney nodded.

Unparalleled musician that she was, Paddie had a finely tuned sense of timing and the ability to communicate to other musicians with a look and a movement. Now, as never before, she drew on those skills. She looked at Whitney the way she would the second before a horn solo was to begin. Then a move of her hand, a slight widening of her eyes . . . and they acted.

Paddie was out first, screaming like a banshee and flailing her poker, and then came Whitney, calmly pointing her revolver at the two men. One was balding and heavyset, with a mustache that needed trimming. The other wore overalls with no shirt and was one of the largest individuals Whitney had ever seen.

He was the one with the gun.

A man built like Harry Stagliatti lay face down in the sand, but Whitney forced herself not to look at him.

"Drop it," she told the huge man.

He stared at her. "What the hell—"

"The gun," she said stoically. "Drop it."

The words came just as she realized that if she hadn't mentioned the damn thing, he might not have remembered he had it until too late. As it was, he looked at the gun, grinned, and pointed it at Whitney.

But it was the balding man with the mustache who spoke. "No one wants any trouble, ladies," he drawled patiently. "So why don't we just be on our way?"

His comrade in thuggery and Paddie both protested, but Whitney and the fat man knew a stalemate when they saw one.

"For all I care, she can go on and kill you, and you can go on and kill her," the balding man said. "I'm leaving." He spread out his palms in a gesture of innocence and an appeal for common sense. "Ladies?"

"We don't care about you," Paddie said. "Go."

Whitney nodded curtly, her gun and her eyes focused on the fat man.

"Let's go," his friend said, patting him once on his massive shoulder. "We've done enough damage for one night —no point in getting ourselves killed, too."

"I can take both of them."

"Do what you like. I'm getting out of here."

Then he walked toward the truck. The big man looked at Whitney. She wouldn't have met his gaze if she could have avoided it, but she didn't dare avert her eyes for a fraction of a second. What good was one bullet going to do? The man was massive! *If* she could bring herself to pull the trigger, *if* her aim was accidentally on target, there was no guarantee—not even the likelihood—that a single shot from her gun was going to topple him. At least not before he had a chance to pump her slim frame with bullets.

But, muttering obscenities, he finally heaved himself up. Whitney didn't move. Her gun was shaking, but she couldn't help that. Keeping his gun trained on her, the fat man backed toward the pickup, where his comrade had opened the door for him. The truck roared to a start. He climbed in, and they sped off, kicking up sand and dust in their wake.

"That was a close one, Victoria," Whitney said.

"Too close," Paddie said.

"Did you get the license plate?"

"Of course."

They lowered their weapons and stooped beside the squat, unmoving figure lying half under the trailer. "Harry?" Whitney said softly.

"Don't touch me, you maniacs," came the blunt, sarcastic voice of Harry Stagliatti. "Those sons-of-bitches shot my muting arm."

Paddie and Whitney understood at once. Harry didn't

have a right arm and a left arm. He had an arm, which co-incidentally was his left, that held the horn up to his mouth, and a hand, also his left, that operated the three valves and a fourth valve to switch from F horn to B-flat alto horn. He had another arm, his right, that controlled the famous bell of the horn. Just by positioning his hand in the bell, he could adjust to every nuance of pitch and tone, from a soft buzzing mute of a stopped bell to the loud bom-bastic sounds of an open bell. Harry Stagliatti was a mas-ter of these nuances. They were what gave his instrument some of its incredible versatility and was one reason for its being an integral part of both wind and brass ensembles.

So Harry had been wounded in his right arm.

Moaning, he sat up, refusing any assistance from Paddie or Whitney. Blood had soaked through the sleeve of his shirt and was oozing down his hand, but he swore he'd bite the first one who tried to touch him. He called them names and said he had had everything under control.

"Ha," Paddie replied. "They were going to kill you."

"Moron," Harry snapped. He was not a handsome man, but he had a nice, straight nose and a face that he said had character. Like Paddie, looks did not interest him. "I was playing dead."

"Humph," Paddie said. "Then why were they discussing whether to kill you?"

"I was crossing one bridge at a time and— *Ouch!* Damn it. Whitney, don't look at me like that. I'm not dead yet, no thanks to you two. Thought you were a goner for sure, you nitwit. Whatever possessed you to start acting like Wyatt Earp—and where in hell did you get that thing? Looks like a goddamned elephant gun."

Whitney started to laugh. Shocked, Harry muttered in dis-gust. He was a cantankerous, salty-tongued, lovable man, but if it weren't for his arm, she'd have hugged him.

"You're not dead," she said.

"Not for anyone's lack of trying, minx." He attempted a feeble grin.

"What were you doing out here?" Paddie demanded. "You have much to explain, Mr. Stagliatti."

"You want me to talk before or after I bleed to death?"

"Harry's right, Victoria. We have to do something about

his arm. I suppose I could go back to the cottage and get your car—"

She stopped and stared. So did Paddie. Harry cocked his head around and laughed gleefully. "Ha-ha! Here come your just desserts, ladies. Will the real Wyatt Earp please rise?"

Daniel Graham had stepped out from behind an orange tree, one rifle slung over his shoulder, tall, masculine, and not pleased. He clapped his hands three times. "Marvelous show, ladies," he drawled sarcastically. "Marvelous."

"He's the other reason I wasn't too worried about our poacher friends," Harry explained. "Has a capable look about him, doesn't he?"

"The three of you," Daniel said darkly, "ought to be dead."

Paddie sniffed. "I suppose we just spoiled your fun?"

"No. You ran off two men, one of whom was armed, with a poker and an unloaded gun. Believe me, it was not fun to watch. I thought for sure I'd be forced to shoot one of them."

"Shoot . . ." Whitney mumbled, suddenly feeling dizzy as the memory of the huge man with the gun came rushing back to her.

"I wouldn't have let the bastard shoot you, darlin'," Daniel said with his most seductive grin.

"Operas," Paddie muttered.

Daniel ignored her. "I had my rifle pointed right at ol' Fats Gillibrew's gut. Didn't think he was the violent type, but you never can tell about poachers, especially when they're cornered."

Whitney gulped in air and fought the wave of dizziness. *"Why didn't you say something!"*

If possible, his grin broadened. "Wanted to see if you could pull it off, sweetheart."

The dizziness vanished, and in its place came an unreasoning, cold anger. "I could have been killed!"

"I'm a good shot, m'love."

With that, Daniel ambled over and squatted down beside Harry.

"Well, Harry," he said, "I guess we ought to get you to a doctor. In much pain?"

Harry's answer was a series of expletives. Daniel informed him that a true Southern gentleman does not curse in front of women, but Paddie and Whitney were obvious exceptions to the rule. One couldn't *help* cursing in front of them, with them, or at them. Harry responded that the last thing he wanted to be was a Southern gentleman.

Daniel laughed and told them all to stay put while he fetched his Jeep, which was parked on a narrow road about five minutes away. He chucked Whitney under the chin. "If Fats comes back, darlin'," he said, "don't tell him your gun isn't loaded."

He trotted off into the grove.

"Well, well," Harry said, "I can see you have a lot to tell me, Whit."

"Ditto for you, Harry," she said.

He grinned valiantly, but the contrast of his teeth against his skin showed how pale he was. "My tale won't be half so interesting. Paddie? You're not going to faint or anything, are you?"

"Humph," Paddie said, but wiped something out of the corners of her eyes. They couldn't be tears; Victoria Paderevsky never cried.

Nearly three hours later they were back on Daniel's front porch digging into what passed for breakfast. No one had felt like cooking, so on the way back from the hospital Daniel had pulled into a fast-food restaurant and ordered four coffees and four sausage-and-egg breakfasts. He hadn't asked for anyone's order. Whitney thought the sausage tasted like Styrofoam, but, then, so did the eggs. She also thought if Daniel had a full-time maid they could be eating a homemade breakfast. Daniel, it seemed, didn't care about food any more than Paddie did. Both were wolfing down their Styrofoam. Whitney and Harry exchanged looks of empathy. *They* cared about food.

"You feel all right, Harry?" Daniel asked.

"I'll live," Harry responded ungraciously.

He had gotten the settee. Paddie took the rocking chair, and Whitney ended up sharing the porch swing with Daniel. She had expected him to take his chair, yesterday's morning newspaper still folded under it, but he had plopped down on the porch swing. So she had started to take his chair. He stuck out a foot, tripped her, caught her

by the waist, and hauled her down beside him. Paddie
started humming the prelude to Mozart's *The Marriage of
Figaro.*

Harry had looked to be in more pain than he had any
business being in. The doctor had said he'd just suffered a
graze and stitched him up. He got painkiller, but no enzymes. Fortunately the doctor was a friend of the Grahams
and believed whatever story Daniel told him. In any case,
the incident wasn't reported to the police.

When they'd finished their breakfasts and deposited the
nonbiodegradable remains into the biodegradable bag in
which they came, Daniel gave the swing a little push with
his foot. "These ladies are going to bust a gut if we don't
start explaining, Harry."

"Would serve them right."

"You've no room to talk," Daniel pointed out mildly.
"You had no business taking on a couple of poachers."

"I didn't take them on, mister," Harry countered. "They
took me on."

"Be that as it may, shall we explain?"

Harry shrugged. "Suits me fine, but they're not going to
like it."

"They've done a few things I haven't liked, either," Daniel said dryly.

"Paddie, my dear, I've known since the beginning that
you're in some kind of trouble," Harry said. "I intercepted
one of your threatening phone calls and didn't like what I
heard—not one damn bit."

Paddie turned purple. "And so what business is it of
yours!"

Harry calmly scratched his cheek. "I decided to make it
my business."

Whitney suppressed a laugh.

Knowing Paddie as he did, Harry went on, he knew she
would never go to anyone for help—and knew if he offered
his help she would only refuse, get all insulted, and become even more closemouthed.

"You are already on a very thin and frayed rope with
me, Mr. Stagliatti."

"Good," Harry said.

Paddie folded her arms, and Whitney thought she looked
embarrassed . . . and perhaps a little bit pleased.

"So what I decided to do," Harry said, "was to get out from under this damned tyrant's schedules and demands for a few days and see what I could find out."

"What you did was humiliate me by walking out of my orchestra," Paddie grumbled. "You're a big help, Mr. Stagliatti."

"It's Harry, you ungrateful wretch."

"Humph," Paddie said.

Daniel rubbed his chin and mouth, but Whitney could see the edges of the smile he was trying to hold back. Even as exhausted as he had to be, he maintained his sense of humor. And, she thought, his irresistible and powerful sensuality.

"And my resignation humiliated me, not you," Harry went on with feeling; like Whitney, he said what he pleased to Victoria Paderevsky. "I'm the one who walked out."

Paddie folded her arms and rocked viciously in her chair. "So you could get yourself killed."

"My, my," Harry said with a sudden grin, "so the woman does care."

Whitney was losing patience and started humming the prelude to Mozart's *Don Giovanni*. Daniel looked at her as though she were some kind of lunatic, but Paddie at least stopped rocking.

Harry resumed his explanation. Since he didn't expect to stay with the CFSO beyond the opening series of programs—

At this point Paddie interrupted once again, letting loose with the sort of bellow one would expect from a wounded hippopotamus. "You agreed to stay with me one year!"

"And you believed me?" Harry laughed.

"I could sue you!"

"So? Sue."

He resumed. He had brought only the few necessities to Florida with him and set himself up in a residential hotel with what he referred to as blue-haired pastel widows. "They all had cats," Harry said.

Harry Stagliatti was not a cat lover. For years he had called Whitney's parade of cats unspeakable names. Wolfgang, he maintained, was the worst of the lot.

Daniel stretched his arm over the top of the swing and said in a low voice of warning, "Get on with it, Harry."

Whitney missed Harry's rejoinder because she was thinking about the forearm brushing against her shoulder. She didn't think she had moved, and she hadn't noticed that Daniel had moved, but somehow their hips had come into contact.

"I took a change of clothes," Harry said, "bought necessary gear, and camped in the grove, close enough to Paddie's cottage to keep an eye on her, but far enough away so she wouldn't trip over me—and, of course, I knew my way around the auditorium, so there was no problem watching her there."

He had expected to trap whoever was harassing Paddie within a day or two and return to his position in the orchestra, but the "crafty devil" was elusive. He did not expect Whitney to show up as his replacement—"I thought this close to opening night Paddie would show some sense for a change and promote from within"—nor did he expect to run into poachers.

"Victoria thought you'd been kidnapped," Whitney said.

Harry grinned. "Did she?"

Daniel's arm stayed comfortably stretched across the back of the swing. "I'm glad you all think this is amusing," he said dryly.

On Thursday night, while Harry was debating how to trap Paddie's harasser and get back to leading a reasonably civilized life, he heard a horn playing and recognized his very own warm-ups. "Thought I'd gone bonkers," he explained. That was when he realized Whitney was camped out up the grove a piece from him.

"Daniel said I sounded like a dying cow," Whitney put in, at which point Daniel playfully squeezed the curve of her shoulder.

"You did," Harry said.

Whitney sniffed. "It had been a long day."

Paddie rose to her defense. "Warm-ups are not to show off the skill of the hornist," she remarked with her finest grandeur.

"Be glad he found you first, Whit," Harry said. "Thought the crazy son-of-a-bitch was going to blow my head off."

Daniel laughed, totally unrepentant. His laugh made Whitney even more aware of their seemingly innocent physical contact. Her pulse was beating faster, and it had nothing to do with Harry's tale. "Two horn players in one night was more than I could handle," Daniel said.

Their words sunk into Paddie's consciousness before Whitney's. "You knew!" she shrieked, leaping to her feet.

The words sunk in, and Whitney glared at Harry and then up at Daniel. "Daniel Graham, you knew all along that Harry hadn't been kidnapped!"

"That's right," he replied evenly, "and if you two sweet ladies had told me you suspected he was in danger, I'd have reassured you."

"But you *knew* what we suspected!"

"Idiots!" Paddie wailed. "I am surrounded by idiots!"

"Sit down, Paddie," Harry commanded, "before you give yourself a heart attack. Haven't you figured out by now no one listens to your rantings and ravings? We all know you're just a big pussycat. Now sit."

"No one likes me," she stated firmly, but sat.

Whitney was still glaring at Daniel, although his devilish smile and the feel of his hard body against hers didn't help. "Why didn't you tell me?"

It was Harry who replied. "Because I had asked him not to. Before I left the orchestra, I explained my position to him, told him what I intended to do, and he agreed."

"This is outrageous!" Paddie fumed.

"You mean he knew from the *beginning!*"

"Well, yes, of course," Harry said. "I said I was going to keep an eye on Paddie. I don't think he expected me to camp out in the groves, but I had to contact him when I ran out of clothes—"

"Then that explains the hotel!"

"Ah," Daniel said.

Harry looked blank. "What's this?"

"Victoria saw Daniel coming out of your hotel room with some of your things and assumed—concluded, I mean—that he'd kidnapped you."

"I merely entertained the possibility," Paddie clarified.

Daniel laughed. "So that was it."

Whitney pursed her lips. "You could have told me everything, Daniel, but you didn't trust me."

"That's right, darlin'."

His hand slipped around her shoulder, and he twirled a stray curl on one finger. Whitney noticed that Harry was watching with great interest. He would, she thought sourly.

"Mad?" Daniel asked in such a delicious drawl that Whitney could feel her insides melting.

"Furious," she replied, but her grin gave her away.

Harry continued. Daniel had agreed it wouldn't do any harm to have someone looking out for Paddie—at which Paddie humphed—but warned Harry to keep a low profile and stay out of trouble. As with Whitney, however, trouble had a way of finding Harry. On Friday, he was lurking about in the auditorium, keeping an eye on things, when his star pupil sneaked in.

"She was going to see me," he said, and floundered.

Whitney kicked the swing back. *"Harry!* That was you?"

The swing hit the wall, but Daniel stopped it with his foot. "Temper, darlin'," he said languidly.

"You stay out of this, Daniel Graham! Harry Stagliatti, you threatened me with a gun and knocked me down."

"It was not a gun," Harry replied, almost sheepish. "It was a mouthpiece."

Daniel burst out laughing. Even Paddie looked amused. Whitney, however, crossed her arms and blew the hairs on her forehead. She would have kicked the swing again, but Daniel had it anchored with one foot. The other foot rested on his knee, a position which seemed to require his hip and thigh to push more firmly against Whitney's hip and thigh.

"As for pushing you," Harry went on, "I didn't mean to push so hard—didn't think you'd lose your balance quite so easily, but I suppose Daniel has that effect on you. In any case, I knew he'd take care of you."

"So you slunk off."

"As quickly and as adroitly as I could manage."

She huffed.

"Look, Whit, it just wouldn't do to have had you see me just then."

She huffed again.

"Be mad, then."

"She will," Daniel said genially. "She enjoys it, I think."

"What about hitting me on the head?" she snapped.

Harry looked serious. "I didn't do that, Whit."

"And you didn't see who did?"

He shook his head.

But he had conferred with Daniel, and together they decided Harry should remain "undercover" for a while longer. Obviously, whoever was harassing Paddie was getting serious. If Daniel could talk her and Whitney into going to the police, he would, but he didn't hold much hope of that. But someone had to keep watch on Paddie in case she was attacked. Daniel would contact Harry that night, and they would make plans. So Harry had gone back to his tent, which he moved periodically, and prepared to spend yet another night in the Florida wilderness.

"Expected a damned crocodile to move in with me at any moment," he muttered.

Daniel glanced down at Whitney. She grinned and said, "Alligators, Harry. Florida doesn't have crocodiles."

"Just every other kind of pest and pestilence."

Daniel laughed.

During the course of the night, however, instead of coming across Paddie's harasser, Harry had stumbled upon the little band of poachers. He was shot trying to "get the hell out of there." Once wounded, he had every confidence that Daniel would rescue him.

Instead, Paddie and Whitney had.

"Thought I was done for," he said with feeling.

Paddie scowled. "It seems to me," she said in the biting, falsely patient tone she used to cut an undisciplined player to ribbons, "that you two gentlemen have an unenlightened view of women."

"Who the hell said anything about women?" Harry protested. "I'm talking about you and Whit."

"Daniel," Whitney said tartly, "if you keep laughing I'm going to get up and move. You're jiggling the swing."

"You should have confided in us," Paddie declared.

"And vice versa, toots," Harry declared.

Toots? Now Whitney started to giggle.

It was then that Daniel decided their conference had gone on long enough. Insisting what they all needed now was some rest, he dispatched Paddie and Harry to the cottage. "Now that we've 'confided,' he can sleep on the couch—or wherever."

Paddie looked appalled.

"What about Whit?" Harry asked, not looking the least appalled.

"She'll remain here."

"Just remember," Harry said, rising, "her lips are her future."

"I'll do my best," Daniel replied, straight-faced.

Chapter Ten

AFTER Paddie and Harry had gone, Daniel stretched out his legs and gave the swing a little push. "You want to stomp off, darlin'?" he asked lazily.

"No," Whitney admitted, "I'm too tired to stomp."

"Head hurt?"

"Feels fine."

"Mad?"

"I guess we both deserved what we got."

"Want an apology?"

She smiled up at him. "I thought that was my line."

He laughed. "Why don't you blame Paddie and I'll blame Harry?"

"Sounds good to me."

"You care about Harry, don't you?"

"We go back a long way."

"He cares about you, too, although I must admit he has a peculiar way of showing it."

"I know," she said softly. "I guess I always have. Look, you must be exhausted. You don't have to sit up and talk to me."

"You must be exhausted, too, darlin'."

His deep, sexy drawl seemed to vibrate in the small of her back, and lower, until she was tingling all over and was aware only of the man beside her. Harry, Paddie, guns, questions, danger—they all faded into her subconscious. Even remembering his comment required a concerted effort.

"I suppose I am," she said, a little too breathlessly, "but I don't think I could sleep right now."

He pulled his arm off the back of the swing and touched

her chin with two fingers, then curved his thumb along her lower lip, tracing it gently, his eyes searching hers. "Me neither," he said, his voice low, his half-smile seductive. "There are alternatives, m'love."

She nodded, struggling to think beyond the touch of his fingers. "We could take a walk," she suggested.

He laughed softly. "That's not exactly what I had in mind." His fingers moved upward, stroking the corner of her eyes, pushing back the hair on her forehead. "Whitney." His voice was quiet, serious. He wasn't teasing or laughing now. "I've faced danger lots of times—snakes, gators, accidents, occasionally some jerk with a gun. But I've never been as afraid as I was this morning."

"You didn't act afraid," Whitney said wryly, trying not to acknowledge the depth of feeling he was arousing in her. Operas, she thought.

"Anger often follows on the heels of fear. Whitney, I didn't want to lose you. I think the worst kind of fear isn't when your own life is in danger, but when the life of someone you care about is in danger. That's you, darlin'. I care about you more than I've wanted to admit." He smiled, his eyes gleaming. "A damned Yankee French horn player with big blue eyes and a penchant for trouble."

"Must be fatigue," she said as lightly as she could manage.

"Must be." His smile grew tender; his fingers trailed down through her hair. "Either that or I'm falling in love with you."

There was no opportunity to answer, even to think of an appropriate response. His hand dropped to her shoulder and drew her to him, and as she looked into his eyes, their mouths met, opened, gave. The last, lingering stiffness of tension left her body. She relaxed. She melted. She let herself feel and enjoy and respond to the sheer sensuality of Daniel Graham.

"Come to bed with me, Whitney," he whispered hoarsely, "come to bed with me . . ."

And then he hopped lightly off the swing, turned on his heels, and went into the house.

Whitney gasped for breath, but she wasn't confused, not at all. Before they found themselves at the point of no return, he had given her the opportunity to make up her own

mind about what she wanted to do. Possibly it would have
been easier if he had made up her mind for her. Then, if
she had any regrets, she could blame him.

Regrets? Impossible. She debated her next course of
action for approximately five seconds. Should she or
shouldn't she? She should. She wanted to. She needed to.

To be honest to him, to be honest to herself, she had to.

He was coming out of the bathroom when she entered
the bedroom. His white towel was around his neck. The
dark hair on his chest glistened with dampness. The
muscle definition in his calves, thighs, torso, and arms
only added to the sense of power and masculine grace
Whitney felt whenever she was around him, but especially
now. He grinned and with the end of the towel stabbed a
trickle of water from his hair. Obviously he wasn't embarrassed. But, strangely enough, neither was Whitney.

"That was quick," she said, sitting on the edge of the big
bed with one knee tucked under her.

"Cold showers usually are."

His voice was liquid, deep, as seductive as a caress. She
smiled. "You were that sure I wouldn't come?"

"No. I thought it a prudent move even if you did come."
Tossing the towel on the floor, he sat beside her. "Whitney,
Whitney," he said, looking into her eyes, smiling, and
gathered her into his arms.

His skin was cool and damp, firm under the skimming
moves of her fingers, erotic to touch and smell. She
breathed in the fresh aroma of him and teased her tongue
with the sensual taste of him. He lifted her shirt out of her
jeans and spanned her waist with his hands. She was lying
beside him.

"Raise your arms, love," he whispered, "so I can get this
thing off. I want to see all of you."

She murmured something unintelligible, but agreeable,
and raised her arms. Her senses were filled with him. This
was right, she thought. He was right.

The shirt went quickly. He found the front clasp of her
bra, and it followed the shirt. "I can see your heart beating
here," he said, and his tongue flicked out against the pulse
in her throat. He laughed softly, sensually. "It's quicken-
ing." His palm covered her breast, his thumb catching the

nipple, circling it, his mouth still against her throat. "Faster and faster . . ."

She moaned softly, feeling her insides tighten and melt, tighten and melt, pleading. "Daniel . . ."

Slowly he moved downward, taking her nipple into his mouth, covering it was a warm, delicious wetness. His tongue flicked out against it. She arched under him and cried out. His hands caught her about the buttocks and drew her against him, holding her there until they both moaned softly with wanting.

Her pants went then, and her underpants, and he eased himself onto her.

She could only speak his name in reply, and open herself to him, relying upon her body to articulate what she, aching and impassioned, could not.

"You're all I need," he rasped, and came into her, thrusting hard, moaning softly, and then whispering her name over and over.

Whitney responded with her body and soul. They were united—not two halves of one person, but two separate individuals who were giving to each other, receiving, offering, sharing, feeling. Nothing like this had happened to her before. Never. There was no ache but that of passion, no second thoughts, no fear. There was only Daniel Graham. Her mind and body drank in the sight and feel of him, exulted in his every fervid murmuring, answered each thrust, each caress, each burning, arousing touch.

When they reached the threshold, it was she who cried out first, and then again, and then again, until her mind and body were one, and all she knew was the thrill and promise of that moment. They were crossing into new territory. They were creating a world, discovering a star, soaring together off into space, hand in hand.

"Oh, Whitney," he said hoarsely, "oh, darlin'. "

And he laughed, and so did she, and then they nestled together, her heart beating against his, and slept.

Whitney awoke first. She disentangled herself from Daniel's long limbs, tiptoed downstairs, and indulged herself in a warm bath. Reality had an unkind way of presenting itself as she dusted her back and stomach with a mixture of cornstarch and talc.

Daniel Graham was upstairs asleep. He grew oranges and grapefruits and a few lemons in central Florida. He was vice president of a national citrus corporation. He was handsome. He was thrilling.

"And I'm hopelessly in love with him," she said to herself, sighing.

She was a French horn player from Schenectady. She had commitments to three different ensembles, two as a hornist, one as a conductor. People were counting on her. And she liked her work. She liked her little house on the Mohawk River. She was close to the Adirondacks, close to New York City, close to everything she needed and wanted.

Except Daniel Graham.

And now that Harry was back and he and Daniel were both aware of Paddie's problem, there was no excuse for Whitney to stay in Orlando.

Of course, if Harry's wound prevented him from performing . . .

It wouldn't.

"Harry, Harry," Whitney mumbled, "how would I ever explain you to Daniel?"

It was best, perhaps, not even to try.

Reality, she decided, was not a pretty thing. She put on a pair of rugby pants and a Tanglewood T-shirt and took her horn outside, walking barefoot through the grass to the wooden lawn chairs down by the lake. It was a warm afternoon, sunny and green, a perfect spring day, the sort of day Schenectady would have a couple of months down the road. She dragged a chair out from beneath the table and sat down under a dogwood. The seat was too low and slanted down in back, but Whitney figured she could make do. She scooted up to the edge of the seat, anchored her feet in the grass, and took out her horn.

She did warm-ups for about an hour, then some exercises. Since she hadn't brought out her music and collapsible music stand, she had to do things she had memorized, which was no problem. She had a good memory. She breathed deeply and played her best.

She did not, she thought with some amusement, sound like a dying cow.

And reality began to look less dreadful and lots more bearable. It was more fun to be in love, with all its emotional upheaval and obstacles, she concluded, than not to be in love.

Besides, what choice did she have? Daniel Graham had staked his claim on her heart. There was nothing she could do about it—nothing she wanted to do.

She ran her tongue over her mouthpiece and argued that she ought to be reasonable. How could she be in love? She'd known the man less than a week, and during the course of that time she had thought him capable of kidnapping Harry Stagliatti, harassing Victoria Paderevsky, bonking Whitney McCallie on the head, and doing untold other nasty things. It did not make an auspicious beginning to a love affair.

"I'm just infatuated," she muttered to herself, and opened up her spit valve.

The man had proved himself as thrilling and skillful a lover as she had anticipated. But instead of satisfying her curiosity, their time together had only whetted her appetite for him.

"See?" she said aloud. "A physical infatuation."

Then why did her heart ache when she thought of his smile? Why did her thoughts and fantasies include not just images of lovemaking, but of talking, working, and just being together? A physical attraction was only part of what she felt and imagined and hoped for.

"So I'm emotionally infatuated, too."

And before she could think of an answer to that not particularly erudite comment, she stuck her horn back to her mouth and played the opening solo to *Till Eulenspiegel's Merry Pranks*. Richard Strauss's music may have made an odious contribution to late nineteenth-century German politics, but he wrote incredible horn parts.

She was belting out the crescendo when, behind her, there was the sound of an engine starting. She whirled around in time to see Daniel Graham's Jeep speeding down the driveway.

"Daniel!"

But he didn't stop. Horn in hand, she ran to the edge of the driveway, but he was already careening off, the Jeep's rear tires kicking up sand in their wake. She saw him make a sharp right-hand turn. As she had learned her first night in Florida, Graham Groves was a spider's web of roads. Only the parking area at the back of the house was blacktopped. She tried thinking of where that particular road might lead instead of thinking about how abrupt Daniel's exit was, and how cruel, and, most of all, of how alone she suddenly felt.

"Maybe you woke him up with your practicing," she said, remembering he thought her warm-ups sounded like a dying cow. "And then again . . ."

She went inside to pour herself a glass of orange juice and think.

There was a note on the kitchen table: "Gone to have a talk with FG. Back soon. Stay put and don't scare off all the wildlife with your practicing. D."

FG?

"Who in blazes . . . *Fats Gillibrew!*"

Daniel had gone to confront a man who had nearly killed Harry and had had every intention of killing her! Without backup. Without consulting her or Harry or Paddie. He'd just taken charge of the situation and gone off without them.

She almost pitched her horn across the room. That won't do, she thought; falling in love does not include destroying one's livelihood. So she picked up the vase in the middle of the table and threw *it* across the room.

There was no Fats Gillibrew in the Orlando phone book or any of the other phone books Daniel had. There was also no Fats Gillibrew in his executive Rolodex and no Fats Gillibrew in the leather address book in his secretary.

Obviously, Fats Gillibrew was not an ordinary and wholesome Florida gentleman.

She dialed Paddie's number at the cottage. After ten rings, there was still no answer. Paddie's acute sense of hearing was notorious. Even if she was asleep, she'd have woken up after the first couple of rings.

It was four o'clock on a gorgeous spring afternoon. Maybe she and Harry had gone for a walk. Or maybe they'd gone out for groceries.

Or maybe Daniel Graham had cut down some little road and picked them up at the cottage to go talk to Fats Gillibrew with him.

Or maybe Fats Gillibrew had paid a visit to the cottage and finished up what he'd started.

Or—

"This isn't doing you or them a damn bit of good, Miss McCallie," she said to herself.

So she stormed to her bedroom—or the guest room, since she had already begun to think of Daniel's room as hers, too—and put her horn away. After a few aggravated moments looking for her sneakers, she remembered they were still upstairs. So she stormed upstairs.

And stopped dead in the doorway.

The sheets were rumpled and askew. Her clothes were tossed hither and yon. Daniel's white towel was hanging off a bedpost. She breathed deeply, remembering.

Yes, she thought, I am in love with that man.

"The sneaky old goat."

And then she seized her sneakers and ran downstairs.

Chapter Eleven

Whistling Beethoven's Symphony No. 7, Whitney followed the path around the edge of the lake. By the time she cut off onto the road to Paddie's cottage she was sick of the smell of citrus blossoms and wished she had brought along a gun. The sweet scent reminded her of mint juleps and sleepy afternoons and things romantic. The thought of a gun reminded her of Fats Gillibrew and her own vulnerable solitude. It was quiet in the grove. The bees hummed, the birds chirped, the fish and whatnot splashed in the lake. Every sound was a potential Fats Gillibrew.

But Daniel was supposed to be with Fats. Why was she so worried?

She stopped in the middle of the road. How did Daniel know where to find Fats?

Simple. Daniel Graham had been born and raised in central Florida. This was his turf. She knew musicians, he knew Fats Gillibrews. Daniel could be trusted.

She was just yards from Paddie's cottage when she heard the sound of men laughing. Whitney stiffened, edging her way forward. Harry and Daniel? Were they on the deck drinking mint juleps and laughing it up?

But Daniel had said he was going to talk to Fats!

And it didn't sound like his laughter, or Harry's.

Two men stepped out of the grove, on either side of her. "Don't," Fats warned when her mouth opened to scream.

"Just stay cool," his balding comrade said.

They both held guns.

She nodded. She couldn't have spoken or screamed if she wanted to.

"We've got a problem," Fats said. "And you can help us. Can't she, Carl?"

"Easy," Carl said.

Fats touched her shoulder with the barrel of his gun. "How come you ain't armed this afternoon, eh? Thought ol' Danny would keep you out of trouble?" Fats chuckled, a breathy, oily sound making Whitney want to shudder. "Ol' Danny can't even keep himself out of trouble."

"What do you mean?" she asked sharply.

"Wooo-eee!" Carl laughed.

"Guess ol' Danny's got himself a sweet young thing to look after him—for now, anyway. Maybe he won't live long enough to enjoy you, hmm?"

Fats was a sadistic, ugly bastard, but Whitney decided not to tell him so. "I don't believe you," she said, but her voice was without conviction.

"Then we'll just have to *prove* it to you."

Fats heaved a few chuckles. Whitney could smell the sweat and grime on him. She wanted to move away, or at least to cough and choke, but stood very still. Fats held the rifle up for her to see. "Recognize it?"

Whitney had seen Daniel Graham's rifle enough times to recognize it when she saw it. Feeling herself pale, she nodded.

"Proof," Fats said.

"What have you done with him?" she asked hoarsely.

"Never mind," Carl said.

From their meeting at dawn, she remembered Carl was the more reasonable member of the unprepossessing duo. She looked at him and asked, "What do you want?"

Fats made some filthy comment that caused her stomach to lurch. She wondered what he would do if ol' Danny's sweet young thing vomited all over him. Shoot her? Probably. But what good would she be to Daniel shot?

Carl looked thoughtful. "We need to get into the guest house." He waved his gun in the general direction of Paddie's cottage. "But we don't want any more people to see us than already have. There's two guys sitting out on the deck. We want you to get rid of them."

"Two guys?"

"One's kind of gray and looks like he's got a cob up his ass," Carl said.

"The other's a gook or something," Fats said.

With more control than she had ever exhibited, even when performing at Carnegie Hall, Whitney held back her anger. And her fear. The two men on the porch had to be Bradley Fredericks and Yoshifumi Kamii. She couldn't endanger them.

But what was in the cottage that Fats and Carl wanted so much?

Paddie? Harry?

"There's no need to hurt them," she said, her voice hoarse with tension.

"Not if you get rid of them, no," Carl said reasonably.

"I'll do what I can."

Carl smiled. "Good."

Fats pressed Daniel's rifle against her cheek. It was more frightening and deadly in his hands, a reminder of why she loathed guns so thoroughly. She wasn't embarrassed at all that she was afraid. "If I shoot you from behind a tree or if I shoot you here, it's all the same," he said. "You're dead. Understood?"

She didn't dare nod. "Yes."

They were not just simpleminded poachers. If that's what they had been at dawn, then something had changed them between now and then. Something drastic. Now they were dangerous men. Mean-spirited, sadistic men willing to commit murder. Unless they were just posturing? Overstating their threat so she would cooperate? Perhaps they were as afraid as she.

Somehow she didn't think so.

They prodded her up the road at gunpoint and whispered the things she was and wasn't supposed to do. She was to get Bradley and Yoshifumi into their cars and off Graham property as quickly as possible. She was not to make them suspicious. At every command, she nodded. She wasn't just going to try. She was going to do it. Her life depended on it.

And as they approached the rear of the cottage and Fats disappeared behind a cypress, it appeared so did Yoshifumi and Bradley's . . . and possibly Daniel's.

"We've got enough bullets for everyone," was Fats's parting comment.

Carl held her wrist. They were standing next to an overgrown flower bed at the corner of the house. They couldn't see the deck from their position, and the voices that drifted toward them were low, unintelligible. "Everything'll be all right if you don't do anything wrong," he said.

"I'm to get rid of them and remain on the deck."

"That's right."

"What if they insist I come along with them?"

"Don't."

She nodded. "And then—"

"We'll discuss that afterward. For now you have no choice."

"Daniel . . ."

"He's not here to help you, is he?"

She shook her head, and when Carl gave her a little shove forward, she went.

Bradley almost fainted when she crept out from behind a pine and climbed onto the deck. "Good Lord, Whitney," he said, "where did you come from?"

"Hi." Her throat was so tight she squeaked. She tried a strained, frozen smile. "I was just taking a walk. I thought I heard someone out here. Hi, Yoshifumi."

"We came by to see Paddie," Yoshifumi explained.

"After last night, I don't blame you. She's always had a weird sense of humor."

Bradley pursed his lips. "Poisonous snakes are not humorous."

"I agree, but—" *I'm taking too long! Forget about the damned snake!* "It wasn't real. I—"

"What do you mean it wasn't real?" Bradley demanded. "We all saw the infernal creature!"

"And smelled it, Whitney," Yoshifumi put in. "We came by to make her tell us what in hell's been going on around here. But maybe we don't have to wait for her. Maybe you know. Whitney, tell us. We're worried about Paddie—and the orchestra. We need her of sound mind and body, so to speak."

"I know." Whitney wrung her hands together and, seeing how white her knuckles looked, dropped them to her sides. She tried another smile. "Look, I have an idea. Why don't we meet for dinner somewhere and talk this over? I can't get away now, but what about in an hour or so?" She swore she could hear an angry rustle in the brush. This wasn't part of her prepping. But they had said to ad-lib, hadn't they? "We can meet at Church Street Station. I've never been and—"

"I think we should wait for Dr. Paderevsky," Bradley said sourly.

Damn you, Bradley! "Well, then, you'll be waiting for quite some time," she said, trying to sound cheerful and completely carefree. "She's gone for the weekend. I'm not sure exactly where she went, but she said she needed to go into seclusion and find her equilibrium, or something like that. You know she meditates, don't you?"

"Whitney, you never could lie for shit," Yoshifumi said. "Come on, what's up? You're nervous and— God, are you all right? For a minute I thought you were going to faint. Here, have a seat—"

"No!"

Then, to make matters worse, a car drove up and parked behind Bradley's Chrysler. Matthew Walker got out and waved. "Hey, what's going on?" he called, a fresh, happy face amid the sourpuss concern of Bradley Fredericks, the dignified gravity of Yoshifumi Kamii, and the paralyzing fear of Whitney McCallie. He wore brightly colored golfing clothes. "Y'all having a party and didn't invite me?"

Whitney moaned and gave a plaintive look to the anonymous brush and trees behind her. How was she going to get rid of all three men? Why didn't Carl and Fats just cut their losses and hightail it out of there?

They all greeted each other in a spirit of orchestral fellowship. Whitney, per her instructions, remained standing on the north rear corner of the deck. If she sat down, she would be shot. If she moved in front of or behind someone, she would be shot. Matthew pulled out a chair and nodded to her, but she shook her head.

"I can't stay," she said, "and—um—sorry, but neither can you three. I don't want to sound like a brown nose, but I promised Paddie."

"Something up?" Matthew asked; Yoshifumi explained what they were doing there and about Paddie's skipping out for the weekend. "Sounds like a good idea to me," Matthew said. "Our fearless leader probably could use a rest. What about you, Whitney? Going to tell us what our chairman of the board won't?"

"Yes. *Gladly.* At six o'clock at Church Street Station—Rosie O'Grady's, isn't that one of the places? I'll be there. Right now *I* have to go, and so do you."

"Daniel going to get mad and wallop you if you don't get back?" Matthew was grinning, not at all serious, but still Whitney took offense. "Don't look so serious, sweet pea. I'm just jealous."

He laughed, and she couldn't help but be charmed. "I'm flattered," she said truthfully. "But—"

"But we're cramping your style." He rose, beckoning the others. "As you wish, sweet Whitney."

"She won't tell us anything until then, anyway," Bradley grumbled.

Yoshifumi moved toward her and patted her on the shoulder.

"You all right?" he asked.

"Yes, fine. Just tired. I—I'm not used to all this warm weather and fresh air. But it's nice."

"Nervous about taking Harry's place?"

"I guess."

"Need a ride up to the house, Whitney?" Matthew asked. "I thought I'd stop by and see if I could have a talk with Daniel."

How to explain Daniel was supposed to be having a talk with Fats Gillibrew, but wasn't? "Thank you," she said, smiling tightly, "but no. I need the exercise. Perhaps I'll see you there."

He grinned magnanimously. "Perhaps."

And they left. First Matthew because he was blocking the driveway, then Yoshifumi and Bradley. They all waved. She waved back. Her stomach hurt. Her head hurt. She had to stand as rigid as a steel post to keep herself from screaming out to them for help. Then they were gone in a cloud of dust, and she realized she could stand on the corner of the deck and await her fate, or she could do something.

There simply was no choice.

In one wild, ungraceful move, she leaped forward, knocking down a grid chair, and dashed into the cottage. Two shots rang out in quick succession, then another. She screamed, slamming the door shut and barricading it with a folding chair, sobbing.

"I don't know what to do," she cried, "oh, God help me, I don't know what to do!"

"You can start by getting your ass down," came a low, furious drawl.

She flew around. "Daniel!"

"Get down, damn it!"

She fell to her hands and knees and crawled into the living room. Daniel was crouched at eye level with the sill of the window overlooking Fats Gillibrew territory. He had a revolver in his right hand. His left shoulder drooped down at an awkward angle. She crept up to him. "Daniel?" she whispered. "What's happening? Are they out there—"

"Shh."

She swallowed her next question. He was breathing hard, almost laboriously, with anger, she thought. She touched his left shoulder in a gesture of solidarity, but something warm and sticky adhered to her fingers. She spread them in the light and saw the blood.

"Oh, my God, Daniel—you've been shot!"

"Knifed," he said tersely.

Then he turned and gave her a lopsided grin. She saw the bruise spreading across his forehead and held back a cry.

"Don't faint on me, darlin'—not that you would. More likely to make someone else faint. You're worse than a goddamned rattlesnake. Wish I had another gun for you, but I was relieved of my rifle. Stay close, sweetheart. If worse comes to worse, we can die together."

"We aren't . . . they aren't . . ."

"We'll be just fine, m'love, if Paddie and Harry, sensible and obedient people that they are, get back here in time with the police."

"The police? Daniel—"

A bullet shattered a pane of glass above them. Daniel threw his injured arm over Whitney and crushed her to him, letting the glass fall on his back. He gave her an encouraging grin, but his face was white.

"Seeing you made me forget I'm in pain," he said. "The bastards."

Then he shoved Whitney behind a chair, bashed in a window, stuck his gun out, and fired. There wasn't a prayer that he hit anything, but he seemed to feel better.

"Just like 'Gunsmoke,' " he muttered, ducking below the windowsill. "Are you all right, Whitney?"

"I feel like I should be doing something."

"You've already done enough. Damn it, where's the accursed cavalry? I'll bleed to death before— *Aha!*"

Then Whitney heard it, too: sirens. Daniel laughed and blew on the end of his gun. "And not a moment too soon," he said, white-faced but irreverent until the end. "That, m'sweet, was my very last bullet."

And then he collapsed into her arms.

Chapter Twelve

When the police arrived, Fats Gillibrew and Carl were scrambling into their truck. Two officers plucked them out and escorted them to the deck, where they raised their arms in surrender. No problem, officers, they said; they would go peacefully. No, no, they didn't have any guns. They just had the rifle Fats got off Daniel Graham when Daniel had jumped him for no apparent reason. Yeah, they'd fired it; sure. Daniel was shooting at them. Nearly blew Carl's head off! So Fats fired one shot in self-defense. Nobody was hurt, right? Naw, that cut on Daniel's arm wasn't anything; just Carl protecting himself when Daniel attacked.

"Seems Mr. Graham got the short end of the stick, boys," said the police officer in charge, a ruddy-faced man with gray hair and dimples.

"That's his problem," Carl said. "Weren't our fault."

"What were you doing on his property?"

If Fats had weighed one or two hundred pounds less, he might have actually looked sheepish. "Just took a wrong turn, that's all."

Daniel cast an oblique look at Whitney. He was seated in one of Paddie's grid chairs and looked remarkably fit for a man who'd been knifed in the shoulder. His white cotton shirt was bloody and torn. Whitney felt a twinge of guilt when she found his poor battered body as masculine and sexy as ever. At the moment, however, his half-amused, half-sarcastic look did not promote any deep feelings of sympathy. In different company she would have stuck her tongue out at him. She was a better liar than Fats Gillibrew!

146

"Okay," the police officer said, twisting his mouth thoughtfully to one side. "I guess we ought to—" Paddie's 1965 Chevrolet Bel Air, not in mint condition, came to a grinding halt behind the police car. Harry and Paddie hopped out. The gray-haired police officer moaned. "Oh, no, not those two again!" He raised his voice as they approached. "I thought I told you two to stay put!"

"It's advice, Jim," Daniel said with long-suffering patience, "that musicians don't seem to hear."

Whitney made a face. "Naturally you're on a first name basis with the local law," she said.

"Naturally," Daniel replied evenly, looking her up and down with a frankness that jarred her. "Better watch it, love. You already have a lot to answer for."

She smiled impishly. "Oh, really?"

He looked at her steadily. "Yep, really."

"Well, so do you."

He grinned. "Good."

Paddie stomped onto the deck with Harry in tow. He looked a little pale. Paddie, on the other hand, was purple. She waved her hand at Daniel and Whitney and Carl and Fats and even the police as if they were all unwelcome Florida cockroaches. "Peace I want!" she boomed. "Quiet! An environment in which an artistic mind can flourish, and—"

"It's no use, Paddie," Daniel interrupted.

Paddie stared at him, stunned. Whitney wondered if she'd ever been interrupted during one of her tantrums. Harry wiped a grin off his face and cleared his throat. Jim, the police officer, didn't bother, nor did his young brown-haired assistant with the mustache. They both chuckled.

"It's all going to come out," Daniel added.

Paddie paled, but said stoically, "I know."

Daniel was remarkably calm. Perhaps it was loss of blood, Whitney thought. She'd offered to clean him up with some of Paddie's Castile soap and water and wrap a towel or something around him, but he'd told her if she touched him he'd chop her fingers off. She believed him.

"Let me worry about it," he said.

"Bah," Paddie said, and flopped down into a chair.

But not for long. Jim heaved a sigh, muttered something

about the luck of the Irish, and straightened up, looking official. "I'm going to need statements from the lot of you."

Paddie looked at him haughtily. "You have mine."

"Yeah, and I'm going to need it again. I've got some questions to ask all you ladies and gentlemen. This all sounds like one giant mess to me." Not even noticing Paddie's appalled look, Jim turned to Daniel. "You want to see to that arm before or after we start sorting things out, Daniel?"

"After will be fine."

"Hope gangrene doesn't set in by then," Jim grumbled, and motioned for the two police officers guarding Fats and Carl to move them out.

Harry hung back, looking worried. "You all right, kid?" he asked Whitney.

"Yes, fine." She smiled, suddenly wanting to hug him more than she had in her entire life, but Daniel was watching them closely as he climbed painfully to his feet. There would be time enough for other explanations later. "How 'bout you, Harry?"

Harry grinned and gave her a friendly squeeze. "I just keep thinking it's maple sugaring time up on the farm, Whit. I can almost smell the stuff." He winked and let her go, joining Paddie.

Boldly, with a peculiar sense of happiness, Whitney slipped her arm around Daniel's hard waist and helped him balance. "Be a hell of a time to faint," she said, mimicking his lazy, mocking drawl.

"Darlin'," he said in the real lazy, mocking drawl, "you're not helping matters."

"I just don't want you to fall. What would Paddie say? What would Fats Gillibrew—"

"Falling's not what I'm worried about."

"No?"

"No. It's sweeping you into my arms and carrying you off into my grove. We could make love among the citrus blossoms night after night and day after day. No one would ever find us."

"Oh."

"Sounds irresistible, doesn't it?"

"I thought you were angry with me."

"I am—and you with me. Ah, but think of the punishments we could devise for each other."

Jim turned and yelled for them to hurry it up.

"But duty calls," Daniel said. "Your arm, darlin'. Another second with your lithe and lovely body against mine and I'll grab the first vine and swing us out of here."

She removed her arm, and Daniel had the gall to laugh. But then he nearly fell down Paddie's three little steps, and it was her turn to laugh. He scowled up at her, but took her arm. Fortunately, Whitney thought, there were no vines around.

That evening the weather turned cool, and Daniel built a fire in the big stone fireplace in the cypress-paneled study while Whitney put out the last of the spaghetti sauce for the cats. She had heated it up and served it over some hamburger buns she'd found in the freezer. Daniel hadn't made a single disparaging remark, but Whitney had. "Harry would disown me," she muttered.

But Harry, at least, wasn't there to feast on her makeshift cuisine. He was off with Paddie, who was "politicking" for the first time in her career. She'd tracked down all the people who had been in Daniel's living room the night before, told them the bare bones of what had happened, and invited them to join her at a press conference at Graham Auditorium at eight o'clock that evening. Daniel would be there.

Harry said he could think of better things to do on a Saturday night, but if Paddie needed a shoulder to lean on, he'd be there. Paddie, of course, said she certainly did not need a shoulder to lean on, but asked him to be there in any case. Harry agreed. He seemed relieved, but Whitney understood. Harry Stagliatti preferred not to be needed *too* much.

Whitney wasn't sure whether she would go to the press conference. It was a CFSO event, and she wasn't sure she was a CFSO member. It was one of several things yet to be resolved.

She joined Daniel in the study. He was sitting on the floor, his back against the couch, one leg stretched out in front of him, the other bent, his good hand clasped around his ankle. She thought he looked pensive and thoughtful, but, considering what he had been through, she didn't think this unreasonable. The knife wound wasn't deep, but it was painful, and his doctor, who apparently knew him well, warned him against any further heroics for a day or two.

And she had selfishly wondered if "heroics" included lovemaking, and decided probably it did.

Entering the room quietly, Whitney grabbed a lightweight blanket off the back of a chair and went and sat down beside him. The house was big and drafty, and she was surprised at how cold she was. She studied the hard lines of Daniel's face, where the flames flickered in shadows.

"Boo," she said.

He turned and smiled. "Where'd you come from?"

"Schenectady," she replied, grinning, "but I grew up in Manhattan."

"A real city kid."

"Nope. If I were, I'd still be living in Manhattan."

"Parents?"

"Divorced when I was three. I lived with my mother, but I've always seen a lot of my father. They're both musicians. Mother sings, Father plays—or so Mother always says. They're not like your parents at all." That, she thought, was an extraordinary understatement. She grinned. "You'd have moved out of Florida ages ago if they were!"

"Sometimes I don't know why I stay," he said, almost wistful, but then he chuckled softly. "But then who would be around to appall my mother? I have a younger sister in Jacksonville, but she lives according to the family rules."

"Which are?"

"Work hard, make lots of money, and don't make waves."

Whitney stretched out her legs alongside his. Her muscles were sore and tense—and not just the ones she had used in encountering Carl and Fats. She had also encountered one Daniel Graham that afternoon, but on a very different and far more memorable level.

"I would think you work hard—occasionally. And by all evidence, you make lots of money—unless you're living off a trust fund, which I tend to doubt. But as for not making waves . . ."

"Not my style, is it, darlin'?"

"Not from what I've seen."

He grinned, showing no bitterness over his roots. He had been born into a world of family, wealth, and tradition. Whitney had been born into a world of music. They were the givens of their lives, the things they could not change. But they were very different worlds. Geography played a role, but perhaps not the biggest role. There were no orange trees in Schenectady, of course, but there was music in Orlando, the arts, a cultural environment. And Daniel was a prominent patron of the arts. But being a patron of the arts didn't automatically mean he would find any commonality, any happiness or fulfillment, with a musician.

"Your lips do the strangest things when you frown," Daniel was saying. "Is it from all those years of playing horn?"

His teasing brought her out of her somber thoughts, and she couldn't help but smile. "I've developed muscles in my lips you've never even heard of."

"Is that what you think about when I kiss you? The muscles in your lips?"

"Of course," she said lightly. "What else should I be thinking about?"

"Oh, lady, if I weren't a wounded man . . ."

"If you weren't a wounded man, Daniel Graham, I wouldn't be pushing my luck."

He grunted, but she could see the glint in his eyes. And it wasn't just the reflection of the fire. "You've pushed your luck about as far as it'll go, m'love."

"Then I guess it's a good thing this business is finished and done with."

"Yes," he said heavily, and turned flush to the fire, the flames flickering in shadows on the hard lines of his face.

"Daniel . . . it is over, isn't it?"

"You know as much as I do, Whitney."

Which, she thought, all told wasn't much. Despite Paddie's protests, they had told the police everything—about the coffee, the misplaced scores, the switched covers, the phone calls, Harry, Whitney's arrival in Orlando, their discovery of the poachers at dawn. They neglected to mention Paddie's dead snake, and Paddie didn't bring up the cartoon, which meant Whitney didn't, either. In its own way, it was perhaps the nastiest item of all. Jim had not been thrilled with their past reticence. He had told Daniel he ought to know better. Obviously musicians couldn't be relied upon to know much of anything besides Beethoven and Mozart.

While Whitney had been practicing her horn and contemplating her budding romance with Daniel Graham, he had received a panicked call from Harry. The two poachers were skulking around outside and Paddie was getting ready to go after them with her poker. Daniel instructed them to call the police and, if possible, get out of there; he'd be right along. He'd scrawled a note to Whitney—"an exercise in futility," he called it—and left.

After calling the police and debating whether the two men were actually after something or just skulking, Paddie and Harry decided to take their chances. The moment Fats and Carl were out of sight, they raced out to Paddie's car and made their exit.

Fats and Carl meanwhile attacked Daniel before he even got to the cottage. Or, according to their story, he attacked them. Either way, in the scuffle that ensued Daniel was stabbed and lost control of his rifle, but managed to get away into the brush. Fats and Carl probably would have found him, but Yoshifumi and Bradley had shown up and planted themselves on the deck.

And then Whitney had come whistling onto the scene.

"Beethoven, wasn't it?" Daniel had asked sarcastically.

"His Seventh," Whitney had replied blithely. "Second movement."

He had gritted his teeth and resumed his tale. He had overheard Fats's and Carl's talk with her, but there was nothing he could do. Despite all the evidence to the contrary, Daniel didn't think they would go so far as to murder her. Nevertheless, he had crept into the cottage through the back and prepared to provide cover, if it came to that. He was hoping it wouldn't. Whitney would do as she was told, Bradley and Yoshifumi and, as it turned out, Matthew would all leave quietly, and the police would arrive in time to apprehend Fats and Carl.

"It wasn't all as neat as I had hoped it would be," he had said in conclusion, "but we did all survive."

Jim had simply shaken his head in disgust.

Fats and Carl had stuck to their bare bones story. Victoria Paderevsky had rented a cottage that had been unoccupied for several years in, from a poacher's point of view, a strategically located area. That part of the grove was isolated from the rest of Daniel's property, but had good access to a major highway. And it was on the border of Daniel's huge, late-ripening, high-priced Valencia orange grove.

But it was also in Paddie's front yard, and her constant comings and goings posed a threat to the poaching operation. Fats and Carl were afraid she would stumble on them and blow their little business wide open. They wanted her out of the cottage—but how to get her to move? Apparently they thought about it and came up with their little scheme of harassment. Paddie was under a great deal of pressure, she wasn't personally popular, and she was a woman. It would be a simple matter to harass her into quitting her job and leaving town. And, in the bargain, who would blame a couple of poachers when the woman had an entire orchestra that didn't especially like her? There were suspects galore!

Of course, they hadn't counted on Paddie being Paddie . . . or on Harry and Daniel and Whitney.

Whitney pointed out that that was rather elaborate thinking for the likes of Fats and Carl. How would they know to switch covers on a score? "Ask them," she had said. "They probably don't even know what a score is!"

Jim promised he would take care of all that, but Whitney sensed he thought she was maligning Florida men, which was ridiculous. *She* had dealt with Fats Gillibrew and Carl Johnsbury! And they weren't Daniel Grahams. Definitely and decidedly not. It seemed to her—and, of course, she said so—that Fats and Carl were not the ringleaders of their poaching operation.

But Fats and Carl insisted they worked alone and only were stealing fruit from Daniel. Jim mentioned the entire county had been troubled by what appeared to be a fairly organized ring of poachers, but he couldn't say if the two men were part of it or not. He was confident, however, that they would "share some more information with us."

It was how they all had left it. Paddie and Harry had gone back to the cottage, Whitney and Daniel had gone back to the house. On their way out of the police station, Jim had warned them that the press would be calling. Obviously *he* didn't think a few musicians should merit media attention: The world premiere of the Central Florida Symphony Orchestra had been news to him.

"What are you going to do now?" Daniel was asking.

"I don't know," Whitney said, wiggling her stocking-covered feet at the fire. "I guess it depends on Paddie and Harry—Harry, mostly, I would think. If he can't play, of course I'll stay. And . . ." She paused, thinking carefully of what to say next, what she had to say. "And it depends on you, Daniel. Regardless of what Paddie and Harry do, I'll stay if you want me to. This afternoon—this afternoon meant a great deal to me."

Daniel said nothing. The fire crackled. Whitney felt her eyes fill with tears, and hugged the blanket close. The house was big and drafty; her nose was cold. Finally Daniel rose and tossed another log on the fire, then stood in front of it, his uninjured arm on the stone mantel.

"For how long, Whitney?" he asked, not looking at her.

"What do you mean?"

He turned then, one side of his face glowing in the light of the fire, the other dark. "I mean two weeks isn't enough, but I'm not prepared to let you go . . . or to keep you here. 'This afternoon' "—he smiled wryly, sadly—"meant a great deal to me, too. More than I had ever imagined. But it won't happen again, Whitney. It can't. Two weeks just isn't enough time. We're adults. We can stop what we've started."

"If that's what you want," she said simply, holding back the tears.

"Maybe it's what has to be. I don't want to uproot your whole life for a relationship three days old."

"Maybe my life could use a little uprooting."

"You have commitments in New York."

"Musicians are romantics. They'd understand."

"And what's here for you, Whitney?"

"You."

"That's not enough, and you know it."

She attempted a smile. "Maybe we could kidnap Harry."

"That's my Whitney," Daniel said wistfully. "An answer for everything."

"Daniel . . . I've never felt this way about anyone. I know it hasn't been long, but it's right. I want to know you better, but I think—I know how I feel." She bit her lip. "We're both tired. We can talk tomorrow."

His hand dropped to his side, and he looked at her, started to speak, stopped, and walked out of the room. He had a press conference to attend.

As the tears flowed freely down her cheeks, she decided there was no point in her going to the press conference.

Chapter Thirteen

THE press conference was being held in an ensemble room across the lobby from the main concert hall. Whitney sidled up to the open door and peered in. She hadn't changed her mind about not attending; she just wanted to check and see where everyone was. Reporters and two camera crews occupied the near end of the room. In a row of chairs at the front sat the core group of CFSO people: Angelina, Yoshifumi, Bradley, Lucas, Matthew, Thomas, and Rebecca. It was an impressive show of unity.

Paddie was resplendent in bright red and a gaudy necklace. She had the microphone, of course. Beside her, Harry was picking lint off his sling. As far as Whitney was aware, he didn't need a sling, but, knowing Harry as she did, she assumed he had added it for effect.

Standing to the side—tall, impressive, and sober—was Daniel Graham. He looked out at their audience, his eyes narrowed, and automatically Whitney flattened against the wall. It was as if he had sensed her presence. But she didn't want him to call attention to her. If she could have had him at her side now, she would have—but that was not an option. The press conference had to go on without interruption, and she had to do what she had come here to do. Daniel couldn't help her.

"You have my statement, ladies and gentlemen," Paddie was saying. "Now I would be happy to discuss the orchestra."

Whitney wondered if that was the first time Victoria Paderevsky had referred to the CFSO as *the* orchestra instead of *her* orchestra.

"What are the names of the two men apprehended?" a reporter asked.

"This is not for me to divulge," Paddie replied stiffly; she obviously preferred to discuss her plans for the CFSO.

There were more questions of a nonmusical nature. Reporters were much more interested in Paddie's opinions on poachers and harassment than on Beethoven and Stravinsky. Paddie wasn't getting her way, but Whitney was relieved. The press conference wasn't in danger of breaking up any time soon.

She tiptoed back down the hall and out into the lobby. Everyone was accounted for. *Everyone.* She had only to get backstage, perform her little investigation, and slip back out. She'd parked the Jeep near the door so she could make a quick exit. Daniel had taken the Porsche.

The Jeep was not a sensitive vehicle. On her way to Paddie's cottage, Whitney had nicked two trees and run over a scrub pine. Screaming through citrus groves in a Jeep with no suspension to speak of was not her forte. But the experience, at least, had delivered her from the last of her sniffles. They had been foolish from the beginning, she had decided as she'd searched for Paddie's duplicate set of keys. Why was she crying over a relationship three days old? Because she was in love?

Humph, she had thought, quoting Victoria Paderevsky.

Besides which, she thought now, creeping into the dark auditorium, Daniel hadn't wanted to ship her off to Schenectady. He had wanted her to *stay.* It was the details that concerned him. Uprooting her life. Phooey! He was just being honorable.

"And why are you thinking about Daniel Graham now?" she muttered under her breath.

In addition to his Jeep, Whitney had also borrowed one of Daniel's flashlights. He had several in the back room with the washer and dryer, but she had chosen an unobtrusive one about the size of her middle finger. She had even checked to make sure it worked. She had considered taking along a weapon this time, but Daniel's gun closet was locked.

She fished the flashlight out of her jeans pocket and flicked it on. Its thin ray of light seemed pitiful in the vast

darkness of the empty auditorium. But Whitney had ushered at Lincoln Center for years. She would manage.

And finding her way backstage was by far the easiest
part of what she meant to do. The hardest part would come
later, when she had to confront the man or woman who
had drawn the caricature of Paddie and the dozen other
world-famous conductors.

Whatever else remained uncertain and negotiable, that,
in Whitney's mind, did not. Fats Gillibrew and Carl Johnsbury had *not* drawn that nasty little picture. And Whitney
was convinced that the person who had was at the heart of
the events of the past week. Fats and Carl themselves had,
in their overheard conversations, referred to a third person.

And that was who Whitney was after.

She crept onto the stage and wove through the music
stands and chairs. To anyone else, it would have been a
maze worthy of King Minos. To Whitney, it was as intelli-
gible as a set of dining room furniture. She had practically
grown up in an orchestra. She could find her way around
one blindfolded.

Still, her heart was pounding when she emerged backstage. She wanted to turn on a light, but didn't dare. Instead she leaned against the wall and allowed herself one
wish. It was simple enough: Daniel Graham. She wanted
him here, beside her, urging her on, working with her.

Loving her.

But, of course, Daniel would never have let her come.
That, she thought, was something to work out during the
next three days of their relationship. More details.

Now came the difficult part of her self-imposed mission:
She had to find the orchestra library. Suddenly her little
light seemed ridiculously inadequate. She edged forward
down the hall toward Paddie's office, flashing the light on
the doors as she went. Only Paddie's was marked. Her only
consolation was that Paddie's string of keys were all
neatly labeled. Stopping in the hall, Whitney dug them out
and found the one to the library.

She hoped the members of the Orlando media were tena-
cious and Paddie stuck her foot in her mouth.

But she could just see Daniel stepping forward and cutting them all short. "Ladies, gentlemen," he would drawl, "thank you for your time. Good night."

And they would all get up and leave. Daniel Graham had that kind of effect on people.

Daniel, Daniel . . .

No, she said firmly to herself; she would not think about him now. But how could she stop? *Willpower. The same stubborn pride that's kept you playing horn all these years.*

The key fit into the lock on the fourth door she tried. Holding back a cry of relief, she pushed the door open slowly, careful not to make a sound. Then she shut it behind her and flipped on the light.

And felt foolish and sneaky.

The black concert folders were all stacked neatly in boxes. Paddie refused to let program music off the premises, insisting that players, whom she regarded as little more than irresponsible children, use their own or backup copies for practice.

In the folders Whitney expected—hoped, dreaded—to find a clue. A scrap of paper, a doodle, a drawing, a note—something, anything, that would prove to her, if to no one else, that the "business" hadn't ended with the arrest of Fats and Carl. Then she could do what had to be done to protect Victoria Paderevsky from a lunatic still at large in her orchestra.

She began with the violin section.

She discovered that the second violinists had a penchant for trivia games and the trumpet section whiled away long tacets, sections during which their instrument wasn't required, by playing hangman. There were lots of doodles, but none bore any resemblance in quality or subject to Paddie's shredded drawing. Yoshifumi's folder was immaculate. So was Bradley's. Angelina's held a review of a concert she had played in Miami. Lucas's music was dogeared.

Breathing more easily and feeling foolish, Whitney sat back on her heels and wondered if she'd simply been reacting to Daniel's mood. Maybe if he had kissed her, just once, she wouldn't have gone on this wild goose chase. But had she really thought Yoshifumi or Angelina or Bradley or Lucas capable of such nastiness? She didn't, she told herself; she was just entertaining the possibility. And just because she hadn't found anything damning in their folders didn't mean they were exonerated.

Yes, she thought bitterly, now she ought to check the bathroom graffiti.

She was beginning to regret her impulsiveness.

But she had come this far. Why not check out what she could about the other people? Rebecca was head of the Friends of the CFSO Society. Probably she would have an office—

"How can you *possibly* suspect Daniel's mother?" She was disgusted with herself, but dug around on Paddié's string of keys, found one labeled "Friends of Orch." and one labeled "Matt," and set off, wondering if both parties knew the conductor had keys to their offices. Paddie was thorough. Her backup copy of Daniel's office key was also on the string.

Matthew's office was across from Paddie's. It was a small, neat cubicle and—

She froze.

And on the desk was a paper blotter covered with doodles. Not one was of a world-famous conductor. Not one was nasty. Not one was proof that Matthew Walker was anything more or less than a capable general manager of an orchestra.

But they were all Whitney needed to see. They were the same style as the drawing he had left in Paddie's cottage. Could she tear off the top page? Would he notice?

She had to, and it wouldn't matter if he noticed. He had to be stopped. Somehow.

She set her flashlight on the corner of the desk and cleared off the damning blotter.

Behind her, the door creaked.

Gulping in air, she whirled around.

Matthew Walker strolled in, shut the door, and leaned against it. He looked as handsome and charming as ever in his cream-colored suit, but tiny beads of perspiration glistened on his upper lip. "Well, hello."

"Oh, Matthew, hi." Whitney tucked a lock of hair behind her ear and smiled, thinking she was getting much too proficient at smiling under great pressure. She had her hand in the cookie jar, and Matthew knew it. His look wasn't menacing, but she could see he wasn't fooled. He wasn't as tall or as physically impressive as Daniel, but she had a good idea of her own limitations. If she could have burst past him and escaped, she would have by now. She would have to try another of her lies. "I was just doing an errand for Paddie. How did the press conference go?"

"The best snow job Florida will ever see, I'm sure," he said pleasantly. "Daniel saved Paddie from herself and came out looking just peachy. He always does, doesn't he?"

"I wouldn't know. Oh, silly me, I think I'm digging in the wrong box. I suppose this can wait until morning. Paddie's so compulsive."

Matthew smiled indulgently, but the knowing look never left his eyes. "She's not the only one, is she?"

"You mean me?" Whitney climbed to her feet and waved off his comment. "No, only where music is concerned. I'm glad Harry showed up. I've got a beast of a concert series coming up in New York. Lots of modern stuff—you know, with me and my poor little horn dancing over its entire four-octave range."

"It's not going to work, Whitney," Matthew said, his drawl as charming as ever. "You're the prettiest, nicest Yankee I've ever seen, but you're not very good at lying."

"So everyone keeps telling me. Let me help you, Matthew," she said quietly. "It doesn't have to end like this. I know Paddie—"

"It's not Paddie. She's a loudmouthed bitch, but it's not her. I haven't grown up with her. I haven't had to stand back and watch her do everything right. I haven't had to listen to people compare me to her day in and day out. No, Whitney, it's not Paddie."

Whitney nodded, but didn't dare speak Daniel's name. "I know what you mean," she said with understanding. "He can be hard to take, can't he?"

Matthew laughed: a mean, bitter, sad laugh. "Then why are you in love with him?"

"I've only known the man three days!"

"Exactly my point."

He pulled in his lips, not looking half as threatening as Daniel had when he'd hauled Whitney out of his office closet. But perhaps that was part of Matthew's problem. He was charming and sensitive, and he wanted to be neither. Now he was dangerous. Whitney wondered if, for the first time in his life, he had finally gotten what he wanted.

"I never wanted to hurt anyone," he said, and pulled out a gun.

They walked with his right side against her left side. Matthew had Whitney's right arm—her muting arm, she thought with savage humor—pinned behind her back, holding it with his right arm. With his left arm stretched across his chest, he held the gun on her. He guided her out onto the stage. A light was on. She could feel Matthew stiffening as he noticed, too . . . and he wasn't the one who had turned it on.

Whitney didn't breathe or think or hope. She just walked forward.

Then, with a suddenness that only he could manage, Daniel was behind them, jerking Matthew's gun hand.

Whitney cried out in surprise, then kicked Matthew in the knee.

"Damn it, Whitney, don't fight him," Daniel yelled. "Get down!"

The gun went off. She dove, knocking down three music stands, banging her hand, cursing. For a second she thought she'd been shot, but it was just the base of a stand sticking in her side. She jerked it up and leaped to her feet, prepared to bash Matthew.

But she didn't have to. He was crumpled up on the floor, his face buried in his hands.

And he was crying. "I wouldn't have hurt her," he said over and over, "I wouldn't have hurt her."

Whitney set the stand back down and looked up at Daniel. He had the gun, but he wasn't bothering to point it at Matthew. "I know, Matt," he said gently, his voice cracking. "It wasn't Whitney I was worried about. It was you."

Daniel held an arm out for Whitney, and she started to go to him. But a movement in the shadows backstage stopped her. She turned, beyond fear.

Thomas Walker was there, holding a gun, bigger than his son's. It was pointed at Whitney.

"Put the gun down, Daniel," he said. "Matthew wouldn't kill her, God knows, but I will. You can be sure of it."

His eyes never leaving Thomas, Daniel laid the gun on the floor.

Matthew sniffled and looked up, his face red and blotchy. "It's over, Dad," he cried. "Can't you see? It's over. Your worthless son has failed you again."

"Shut up, Matt," Thomas snapped. He was dressed for the press conference: neat and sharp, but his face was filled with anger and contempt for everyone—his son included. "I'm not going to let these people ruin you—or me. Now quit your mewing and get your gun. *Do as I say!*"

"No, Dad."

"Damn it, boy! If only you'd been half the man that Daniel—"

In his outrage, Thomas raised his hand. It was the one holding the gun. Daniel and Whitney saw their opening, but they didn't get a chance to act. In unison, Harry and Paddie stormed out from backstage and tackled Thomas with their bare hands.

"If you treat Matthew with respect, maybe he doesn't act like this," Paddie screeched in her fake Lithuanian accent, pouncing on Thomas.

"I'll be goddamned," Harry bellowed, his tones pure Brooklyn, "if I was going to sit back and watch you slaughter my own daughter!"

Whitney winced. "Harry, you have a big mouth—"

But Daniel was already hooting behind her. "I'll be damned! I'll be go-to-hell damned! You and Harry?" He scooped her up and hugged her to him, laughing. "You're a couple of liars, but I've got you now, Whitney. Oh, but I've got you now."

Chapter Fourteen

THEY ended up taking Daniel and Harry back to the doctor to be restitched. The doctor said he could keep them both overnight and hog-tie them to a bedpost, but Harry threatened to play hunting calls at dawn and Daniel solemnly promised there would be no more heroics. The doctor had taken one look at Whitney and said, "I'll bet."

Then Daniel, Whitney, Harry, and Paddie all drove out to Rosie O'Grady's at the renovated Church Street Station in downtown Orlando and ordered tall, cold drinks. As Harry had said in a simple understatement, they had a lot to talk about. Whitney stirred her drink and looked at Daniel and wondered if she had ever hoped to love a man this much.

"I never knew he hated me," Daniel said heavily. "I never knew."

Paddie shook her head. "Not you, Daniel," she said with a gentleness she usually reserved for her music. "He hated his father, which is a terrible thing."

They all knew who they were talking about: Matthew Walker. The police had taken him away, but he didn't belong with them. They seemed to know it, and treated him gently.

"It's hard to be compared to someone all your life and not grow bitter—especially when it's someone you care about," Harry said.

Whitney choked up. "Pop, that's not why I . . ."

"I know, minx," he interrupted, "but it could have happened. Why do you think I've cooperated with you all these years? You took your mother's name because you wanted to earn your reputation as a hornist on your own, not because your father is Harry Stagliatti."

"Now I'm known as Stagliatti's favorite student."

"And Stagliatti's daughter," he said.

"Humph," Paddie said. "I must have you both for my orchestra. You're bombastic, Harry, but Whitney has a more lyrical style. And a better tone."

"The hell she does!"

"Stagliatti and McCallie—it will be a horn section the envy of the world!"

Harry scoffed. "And how do you propose to find room for my daughter on your roster?"

"I am the music director," Paddie said with great grandeur. "I will find a way."

"I'd rather just quit," Harry muttered.

"After all the trouble I went to to save you from a maniacal kidnapper? You will not quit." Paddie sucked on an ice cube. "I need you for the Strauss."

"You need me, period."

"Yes," Paddie said, and left it at that.

Daniel was looking past Whitney, drinking his bourbon. "I was going to tell you," she said. "It's just—I've gotten so used to not telling anyone."

He smiled. "It's all right, Whitney. I was wondering why you two had the same nose . . . and the same knack for getting yourselves into a mess."

"Now that's the pot calling the kettle if I ever heard it," Harry said. "Paddie, you're right. The man's a tyrant. But better him at the helm than that bastard Walker."

They all knew which Walker he meant. Thomas Walker. The police had arrested him, but his lawyers were on their way before he'd left the Orlando Community College campus. He wouldn't serve much time, if any. After all, what had he done except brandish a gun and make threats?

"His punishment will come from the community," Daniel said, shifting in his chair so that he was almost touching Whitney. "His family has been respected in central Florida for years—and he's ruined their name."

"And his son," Whitney said.

Daniel sighed. "Maybe Matt will pull out of it. He knows what his father is now. I wish I'd seen what was happening, but I simply didn't. I pushed for Matt's hiring as a favor to him—and my parents. They've always known what a boor his father is and were hoping to get him out of his sphere of influence. Then Thomas wrangled a position on the board. He's never had a good thing to say about his son."

"Or anyone," Whitney added.

"That could be me," Paddie said in a strange, quiet voice.

Daniel shook his head. "Not a chance, Paddie. You don't hate people. You couldn't and still be the conductor you are. I'd heard all the rumors, but when I saw you on the podium that night in Amsterdam, I knew the truth."

"Victoria Paderevsky," Harry said, "is mush."

Daniel, Whitney, and Harry all laughed, and even Paddie managed a small smile. But the events of that long day had changed her. In some elusive way, Victoria Paderevsky was not the same woman Whitney had met at the airport just three days ago. But then, Whitney thought, neither was she.

"How did you know I was at the auditorium?" Whitney asked.

"My sixth sense," Daniel replied with an amused half-smile. "I reserve it for a sleek and beautiful cat I know who's used up all her nine lives."

"Meaning?"

"Meaning Mother left the press conference early, saw my Jeep in the handicapped parking zone, and came back to give me hell."

"And you knew what I was up to?"

"Paddie had told me about the drawing just before the press conference. Matt had always enjoyed art—one of his many talents his father both discouraged and belittled. He was there when Mother came in raging about the Jeep. He'd seen me drive up in the Porsche. Unfortunately, he'd gone off before I'd put the pieces together and was able to end the conference."

"I'm glad you did," Whitney said simply.

"So am I," Daniel said, taking her hand in his and placing it on his lap.

She squeezed his hand and rested her head on his shoulder, briefly, before she turned to Paddie and Harry. "What about you two?"

They shrugged. "We just followed Daniel," Harry said.

"Without Daniel's knowledge or permission," Daniel pointed out.

"Yes," Paddie said agreeably, "we could have orchestrated our plans better. However, we did see that filth slink up onto the stage. I should have known what he intended to do."

"But you're just too trusting," Harry commented dryly.

"Yes," Paddie said.

"Like I said"—Harry paused to gulp his scotch and set his glass down hard—"mush."

Whitney, however, refused to be distracted. "What about the poaching?"

"That was Matt, I'm afraid," Daniel said; he still had hold of her hand. "He'd overextended himself financially—something else I knew that didn't point me in the right direction—but couldn't bear to ask his father for help."

"How awful," Whitney said, and smiled up at her own father. "My pop's always been a help—too big a help, sometimes."

"Like when?" Harry demanded.

"Like when you told Daniel my lips are my future."

"Well," he said, "they are!"

"If I was sure you wouldn't follow him, Whitney," Daniel said dryly, but with sea-green eyes twinkling merrily, "I'd send your father off to Vienna to play horn."

Harry snorted. "That's the thanks I get for encouraging you two!"

"No, that will come in another form," Daniel said mysteriously.

"We were discussing the poaching ring," Whitney interrupted when her heart skipped two beats in a row.

Daniel grinned. "So we were. As I was saying, the poaching ring served two purposes: One, it helped him financially; and, two, it helped me look bad. That seemed to be the main motive behind the mind games he was playing with Paddie—make Graham look stupid. I'm sure he didn't think of it until his people pointed out Paddie was mucking up their operation. He'd had me stuffed down his throat all his life. If he could show I'd tripped up by hiring Paddie, then it would build up his own shattered ego. By the way, Paddie," he went on offhandedly, "that's one of the central differences between you and the Walkers: You have a healthy self-image—damned healthy—and they don't. It just came out in different ways. Thomas never had anything to live for, and he was damned if he was going to let his own son find something to live for."

Paddie mulled this over, sucking on another ice cube. "It is sad," she said finally.

"Yes," Daniel agreed.

"So did Matthew bonk me on the head?"

"I don't think so."

"He is not a man of physical violence," Paddie said confidently.

"I think it was Thomas," Daniel said. "Matt had given me a ride to the auditorium, so he was there, but I have a feeling Thomas followed. He'd been at the meeting and probably had figured out that Matthew was behind Paddie's odd behavior and decided to intervene before his son ruined the family image."

"My behavior was not odd," Paddie interrupted.

"Musicians," Daniel muttered, and sighed. "In any case, Thomas must have overheard the three of us talking in the auditorium and decided to take the bull by the horns and at least get Whitney out of the way. He would have seen Whitney and known exactly who he was hitting. If he'd meant to kill her, I'm sure he would have, but then he was bent just on terrorizing her into leaving town. Unfortunately, his plan didn't work." Daniel lifted Whitney's hand to his mouth and kissed it with mock chivalry. "I could have told him it wouldn't."

Harry frowned pensively. "So old Thomas decided he wasn't going to let any upstart female French horn player and bigmouthed female conductor be the ones to ruin his son."

"But why would Thomas go to all that trouble to protect Matthew?" Whitney asked.

Daniel sighed tiredly. "Because Matt's behavior reflected on Thomas. If a man can't produce the kind of son he wants, what kind of man is he? It's cruel, I know, but that's the kind of man Thomas is."

"Poor Matthew," Paddie said quietly. "To have to fit into shoes that are not of your own making . . . it is tragic."

"And I'm sure," Daniel said, "that Paddie's episode with the snake didn't endear her to him. But that's all of it—at least as much as I can make out. I'm not sure we'll ever know all the details for certain."

They were all silent as they drank and listened to the band warming up. Paddie grimaced; she did not like instruments that required plugs. Harry noticed and laughed. "Better get her home fast," he said, taking her by the elbow. "Come on, old girl, we've got to get you in shape for Monday. Ten o'clock rehearsal, you know. Have to get the Stravinsky in shape by Friday." He turned to Whitney. "You know the *Firebird*, don't you?"

She grinned. "You taught it to me, Pop."

"So I did. Now wait till you see what Paddie's done to it." He waved, chuckling, and dragged Paddie off.

"They make an interesting couple," Daniel said dryly.

"Oh, please," Whitney said. "Can you imagine having Victoria Paderevksy as a stepmother?"

"No." Daniel leaned back, smiling, and tucked a lock of hair behind Whitney's ear. "But I can imagine her as a stepmother-in-law. It's one of the many things I'd endure to have you in my life, Whitney."

"Daniel . . ."

"Shh. Let's not talk now. Let's just go home and be together. I love you, Whitney. I've loved you for three days, and I'll love you forever."

She tried to speak again, but couldn't, and he helped her to her feet. Then he winced in pain, and she was helping him. And finally, together, they walked outside and went home.

"Mmm," a deep, sonorous voice was murmuring, "you taste good . . ."

Her eyes closed, Whitney wriggled, but not with discomfort. Something wet and warm was circling her nipple, teasing it with erotic little flicks, making it swell. Something else, firm and slightly callused, stroked her thighs. Must be dreaming, she thought. When they'd turned in last night, she'd insisted on sleeping in the guest room. She hadn't wanted to be responsible for pulling out any of Daniel's stitches. He'd gone off reluctantly, but with a certain cockiness to his step.

Had he had future designs on her?

Sleepily, she realized she was naked. She distinctly remembered putting on her sturdy blue nightgown, more as a reminder of what she was missing than anything else. Daniel's doctor should have talked to *her* about heroics.

"My nightgown . . ."

"Gone," the voice said. "You didn't budge."

Next she realized a man was on top of her. A long, lean, hard man. She reached out with her hands and touched him in appropriate places to make sure.

"Keep it up, darlin'," Daniel said. "We've got all day."

She opened her eyes and looked at him as he kissed his way up to her mouth. "You promised the doctor there'd be no more heroics."

"And I suppose you're going to tell on me?"

She grinned impishly. "Only if you disappoint me."

"I should have known you were Harry Stagliatti's daughter," he said, "by your sharp tongue."

"Shall I slice you to ribbons with it?"

"Please," he drawled, lowering his mouth to hers, "do."

But she didn't. Instead she let her tongue touch and mingle with his and tell him how much she needed and wanted him. She wrapped her arms around the warm, bare skin of his back and drew him down on top of her, stroking his hard buttocks.

"I won't hurt you?" she breathed into his mouth.

He smiled. "Hardly."

And she moved under him, arching to meet his downward thrust, and whispered as he came into her, "I love you, I love you."

"Darlin' Whitney," he said, and then they could say no more. But their bodies spoke. They moved in unison. They were one voice, they were a duet, they were an entire orchestra, they were everything they could think of to be to each other without speaking, without hurting, without smothering. There was only the purity of emotion, and the love they shared.

Afterward, in the stillness of the silent room, Whitney smelled the azaleas and saw the sun and smiled at the man beside her. "Will you teach me to tell an orange blossom from a grapefruit blossom?" she asked sleepily.

"If you'll take me to New York to hear your assorted ensembles perform."

"But, Daniel—"

"You made some commitments, sweetheart. Let me help you keep them. And maybe your groups will inspire me to get something started down here." He propped his head up on one hand and stroked her solid stomach. "I don't want you to have to make all the sacrifices so we can be together."

She was already shaking her head. "I'd have ended up staying in Florida anyway."

He grinned. "I was hoping you'd say that. Harry?"

"Of course. I didn't see much of him growing up and haven't learned half of what he has to teach me and—he needs me."

"And you need him?"

"Yes."

"And me?"

"You're gravy," she said, and, at his immediate and very rude remark, spluttered into raucous laughter.

He swept her into his arms, and with a great display of heroic strength and endurance, made love to her again.

Epilogue

GRAHAM AUDITORIUM was filled to capacity for the premiere performance of the Central Florida Symphony Orchestra. Whitney sat in the horn section next to Harry Stagliatti. Her name was listed in the program as Whitney McCallie Stagliatti. It was, after all, her legal name. That she and Harry were father and daughter wasn't as much of a shock to everyone as she had expected. As Yoshifumi put it, "We all wondered how come you two had stuck by each other all these years." Lucas had simply said, "It's their noses." She wore a long, luxurious, black wool crepe dress that Daniel had insisted on buying her. She had demurred, telling him it was hot on stage, the program was an exhausting one, she'd perspire, she'd dribble spit all over it.

"Stop!" he'd said, laughing. "Must you always be so blunt?"

"Harry has that effect on people. You should hear the things he says to me!"

"And to me," Daniel had replied dryly.

Whitney had grinned knowingly. "Oh?"

"He warned me to leave you a little wind for Friday night."

"The old meddler! He thinks he's so clever. He just keeps looking at me in that way of his and asks if I'm keeping up with my breathing exercises."

"Yes, well," Daniel said, "I suppose discussing spit valves comes naturally to you."

"Don't worry. I'll be demure at the post-concert party with your parents."

"Darlin', just be your easygoing and honest self. It's all I want, all I ever want. You'll wear the dress?"

172

"I'll wear the dress."

"And if you do damage it, we'll just buy you another."

We, Daniel had said. Not *I.* It was always *we.* There was an assumption and a promise in that simple word that Whitney found thrilling. The assumption was that they would be together. The promise was that they would be together not by her fitting into his life or him fitting into her life, but by them building a life of their own, as two individuals with separate thoughts and goals and opinions, and with a love that bound them together.

So she had worn the dress. She had bought her own shoes, however: black ballet slippers. Daniel had groaned in despair.

Harry said she was the envy of the women in the violin section. Whitney told him he looked downright roguish in his black tuxedo. They smiled at each other.

And then Victoria Paderevsky walked onto the stage.

She was dressed loosely and functionally in black, but sometime during the busy week she had had her hair permed, and, to everyone's delighted shock, dyed its original dark brown. For once, she looked her age.

The audience applauded; Paddie bowed and turned to her orchestra.

"Friends," she said, "tonight is for Matthew Walker."

Whitney breathed deeply, feeling the change in Paddie. She had never called her musicians *friends,* and that she would dedicate the premiere concert of the CFSO to Matthew revealed how much his anguish had affected her. For once, Victoria Paderevsky wasn't afraid to be honest to herself.

Then, after a few seconds of silence, the concert began.

In all Whitney's years of playing, there had never been a performance like it. The orchestra played with energy and vigor and heart. The pieces they knew so well—Stravinsky's *Firebird Suite,* Strauss's *Till Eulenspiegel's Merry Pranks,* and, finally, Beethoven's awesome Symphony No. 7—seemed to be drawn from their souls, and perhaps they were. The weeks of grueling practice had assured technical perfection. But tonight, in the darkened, crowded hall, they dared to open up their souls.

And, in so doing, they touched the souls of their audience.

That was the brilliance of Victoria Paderevsky. She knew how to lay souls bare: her orchestra's, her audience's . . . and, most of all, her own.

When she cut off the last dynamic chord of the symphony, she was spent. The tears were streaming down her cheeks. She was breathing hard, but smiling as the audience sat in stunned silence.

"Bravo, my friends," she said to her orchestra, "bravo."

And then the crowd was on their feet, roaring, clapping, and Victoria Paderevsky turned to face them.

Backstage, when the congratulations and the hugs and kisses were over, Whitney packed up her horn in a quiet corner of a practice room. Daniel had promised to meet her at the party if things proved too crazy for him to get backstage. She thought of him now—of the warmth of his sea-green eyes, the strength of his hard body, the depth of his personality. She knew him better after a week, and loved him no less. *Daniel, Daniel,* she thought. Tonight had been for him, too. As she had played, she had felt his presence in the auditorium.

Rising, feeling the ache and numbness of fatigue, she turned, and Daniel was there, stunningly handsome and tall in his black tuxedo.

"You were magnificent," he breathed, and swept her into his arms, his mouth finding hers. "You are magnificent."

She could see the tears still in his eyes and knew that the concert had affected him, too, and not simply because of all that had happened. "It was a good concert?" she asked, smiling widely.

"If the amount of sweat on you is any indication," he said playfully, "it was a fantastic concert."

"Perspiration," she corrected with feigned primness.

"Darlin', when you work that hard for it, it's sweat." He pushed back the dampened tendrils on her forehead and kissed her there, cupping her head in his hands. "I love you, Whitney McCallie Stagliatti."

"And I love you, Daniel Graham." She laughed happily, and laid her head on his chest. "I never want to leave you."

"You won't have to, m'love."

She looked up at him. "That had a knowing ring to it. Are you up to something, Mr. Graham?"

"Harry and I had a talk . . ."

"Uh-oh."

"He was telling me about his farm."

"Uh-huh."

"Says it's a shame no one's there to collect the sap."

"He's never collected sap in his life. Go on."

"Says it's a shame no one's there to feed the chickens."

"He doesn't have any chickens."

"Says it's a shame no one's there to plant peas and spinach this spring."

"Ditto my comment about the sap."

"Says it's a shame no one's there."

"Ah."

Daniel grinned down at her, his arms wrapped comfortably around the small of her sweaty back. The wool dress "breathed" better than any of the cheap polyester dresses Whitney had worn for one or two concerts and tossed. This one could be dry-cleaned and worn again and again.

"But he doesn't want to sell it," Daniel went on. "He says as soon as Paddie falls back to earth, he's going to sweep her off to the Adirondacks for a vacation and a taste of wild currant jelly—"

"Which he will buy at the local country store."

"Whitney, Whitney, you have no faith in your father."

She laughed. "I know him too well."

"In any case, he doesn't expect that to happen until June or July."

"Then he's decided to stay on as principal horn?"

"With the proviso that Paddie hires you as soon as you're available."

"May fifteenth."

"Which brings me back to the farm."

"I beg your pardon?"

"I'm due for an extended vacation. April first through May fifteenth would be nice, don't you think? Springtime in New York."

With a held-back grin, Daniel reached into a pocket and fished out three keys on a length of familiar thirty-pound fishing line. "This key," he said, "is for the front door. This key is for the back door. And this key is for the barn." He palmed all three. "I've always wondered what it would be like to make love in a hayloft."

"There isn't one," she said, her voice strained with emotion.

"Then we'll have to make one."

"Daniel . . ."

"Say yes, Whitney."

"Yes."

He smiled, bringing his mouth down to hers, his breath warm on her face. "You can still be Stagliatti, if you want," he whispered. "Or McCallie, or Graham, or whatever . . . just so long as you're my wife. Marry me, Whitney."

"You have my answer already," she whispered, and affirmed it with a kiss.